fight for us

Copyright © 2026 by Emily Silver®

All rights reserved.

This is a work of fiction. Names, characters, places and incidents are either the product of the author's imagination or are used fictitiously. Any resemblance to actual persons, living or dead, businesses, companies, events or locations is entirely coincidental.

No part of this book may be reproduced in any form or by any electronic or mechanical means, including information storage and retrieval systems, without written permission from the author, except for the use of brief quotations in a book review. For more information, please email the author at Emily@authoremilysilver.com.

NO AI TRAINING: Without in any way limiting the author's exclusive rights under copyright, any use of this publication to "train" generative artificial intelligence (AI) technologies to generate text is expressly prohibited. The author reserves all rights to license uses of this work for generative AI training and development of machine learning language models.

Cover Design by Y'all That Graphic

Editing by Happily Editing Anns

www.authoremilysilver.com

FIGHT FOR US

A Pinecrest, Montana Novel

_____

EMILY SILVER

To the cowgirl in all of us…
Ride free

Chapter One

PRESLEY

"Order up!"

Betty beckons from the kitchen window.

Two steaming plates of fries, onion rings, and burgers await me. Arranging the plates on my arm with ease, I maneuver my way through the tables to drop off the food.

"Let me know if I can get you anything else." I smile at the patrons as they eagerly dig in to their food.

A muffled *thank you* is said as I move on to the next group.

The Hash 'N Hop is the place to be. It's Pinecrest's most popular restaurant. And with that comes all of the more colorful townspeople.

Including the one that just walked in the door. I groan, watching as she makes herself comfortable in the booth by the window.

"Your turn," Rylee says with a knowing smile, standing next to me.

"Didn't I help her last week?"

"No. Because she told me that I was going to get attacked by a bear when I went hiking."

I eye her up and down. "She's usually not that specific. But you do look pretty good for a bear attack."

"Don't I know it?" She slaps my order pad into the center of my chest. "Which means you're up, Pres."

"Ugh. Fine."

I grab the tickets and walk over to the table. Lace fabric is spread over the Formica top with fake candles sitting on it. One large, clear crystal completes her usual setup.

"Hey, Serena," I greet her.

Shifting the purple, gold-trimmed shawl on her shoulders, she turns her gaze, hidden behind large, thick black glasses, to meet mine. Her hair is a wild mess of curls.

"Presley. How are you?"

Her voice carries the same ethereal tone it always does.

"I'm good. How are you?"

I stuff my order pad into the front pocket of my apron and cross my arms.

"Waiting to see what the fortunes tell me about you," she replies.

"Oh, yeah?" I prop my hip against the side of the booth.

She nods. "Yes. It seems they are very chatty when it comes to you."

"Aren't they always?"

She casts an annoyed eye my direction. This isn't the first time I've heard this, and I know it won't be the last.

Two weeks ago, she told me to be on the lookout for something that would hit me in the face. Before that? It was to watch out for snakes.

I always take what she says with a grain of salt.

"I think you'll want to hear what I have to say."

"Alright, what are they telling you?"

She shuffles the tarot cards in her hand, pulling three out. "Oh, yes. Yes."

My jaw cracks as she mutters to herself, tapping a finger on the center card.

The Lovers card.

Great. Just what I needed.

"Have you detached from anyone lately, Presley?"

"Why?" My spine stiffens at her question.

"There's a coldness surrounding this card. Your life is out of balance and there are some issues standing in your way before it resolves itself."

"Right."

"It's nothing to be ashamed about. It allows you to look inside before rediscovering yourself."

"Thanks, Serena. Can I get you your usual?" I grab the pen from my pocket and scribble down her eggs and coffee order that I know by heart.

"Yes." She nods. "I'll have more for you when you come back."

I don't say anything, but stalk off to the kitchen and rip the check from my pad and stuff it onto the turnstile for Betty to start on her order.

It's hard to focus on her words.

"What'd you get?" Rylee asks, pouring a mug of coffee.

"The Lovers."

She winces. "Does she not know you're going through a divorce?"

"Apparently not. Neither does Paul because he won't sign the damn papers."

"Hey." She squeezes my shoulder. "It'll get figured out."

"I hope so." The chime above the door rings out, a new group of people coming in. "Back to work."

The afternoon rush swarms the small diner. With the

fall weather in full swing, Pinecrest is the destination of choice for hikers.

The changing leaves bring everyone to our small town. We have the best trails on the mountains.

Our cozy town is charming, and after a hard day's exercise, everyone comes to the Hash 'N Hop.

Pink leather booths sit under the windows that face the main road. Neon pink lights line the ceiling. High-top stools line the bar with the smell of grease hanging heavy in the air.

"Hi, Arlene!" Chase shouts to the portrait hanging just inside the glass doors.

"There's my favorite customer."

Rylee bounds over to her boyfriend, wrapping her arms around his neck, kissing him hard on the lips.

I sigh. I love that my best friend found love, but sometimes, it stings. With my life in tatters, it's hard to focus on anything but me and my little girl.

Without so much as two pennies to my name—everything is still tied up in my father's estate—I'm working at the town diner.

I enjoy it; I do. It's the longing for stability for the two of us that gets me the most on the hard days.

The chime sounds again, and this time, I light up at the two people walking in.

"There's my favorite girl."

Holding out my arms, I laugh as Poppy leaps into them. "Hi, Mama."

"How was school today?"

"Margo thought Strawberry was dumb to bring into show and tell," Poppy says.

"Really?"

She nods, pigtails bobbing up and down. She's a mini

me—from the bright blue eyes to the blonde hair. Except her smile.

That crooked smile with the dimple she gets from her father.

"I think she was jealous because her stuffed pig wasn't as cool," she says. "What's cooler than a goose dressed like a strawberry?"

"Nothing." I laugh. "Were you at least nice to her about it?"

The last thing I want is for my daughter to be mean to her classmates, even if I don't like Margo. Namely because her dad is friends with Paul, so I know the circles they run in. The circle *I* used to run in.

Her babysitter nods behind her. "The teacher said she was when I picked her up."

"Good. Thanks for bringing her here."

She smiles before leaving.

"I'm glad you were nice to her," I say.

"Yes. I said I liked Strawberry and that's all that matters."

The old goose, dressed like a strawberry and won for me at a fair years ago, has seen better days. But Poppy loves it and sleeps with it every night.

Something else she got from her father.

"That's my good girl." I kiss her on the temple and set her down. "I've got a milkshake for you and then we can head home, okay?"

"Thanks, Mama."

She runs over to her usual spot at the counter and pulls the glass toward her before taking a gulp. Setting Strawberry next to her, Poppy props her up so she can have a sip of the chocolate shake too.

I smile at my daughter, her happiness infectious even from here.

She's the best thing in my life. I don't care how hard it is being a single mom. It's all for Poppy. I'll do whatever it takes to give her a good life. A better life than I had. One where she can do whatever she wants.

With whoever she wants.

Shaking my head, I grab my last order from the kitchen and carry it out. I don't need to be thinking about tarot cards or divorces or my past.

The only thing that matters is moving forward.

Whenever the hell that might be.

Chapter Two

KADE

"You have a meeting at two with Raven to discuss her newest acquisition, and after that you'll need to brief the investors."

"Got it. And all—"

Kelly hands me a stack of papers as we round the corner into my office. "Everything is in here about the company. I made a few notes for you that Raven is worried about that you'll need to discuss with her."

I smile at my assistant as I loosen the tie at my neck. "What would I do without you?"

"Miss the meeting entirely. Do you need anything else?"

"No. Enjoy your lunch. I'll review everything here before my meeting."

She sets another stack of papers down. "Okay. Here's everything needed for the meeting with the investors, including stock options for them."

"It's like you read my mind."

"Can I order you anything for lunch?" she asks, tucking a lock of auburn hair behind her ear, glancing down at the tablet in her hand. "We're trying the new place down the street."

"I'll take my usual salad. Just make sure—"

"There's no strawberries. I know your allergies by now."

"Thank you. I appreciate it. Anything else?"

"Yes." Kelly straightens, looking up, her lips pursed. "Your mother has called again, and I've forwarded you another message from an attorney in—"

"That's all."

My voice is clipped.

She nods. "Let me know if there is anything else you need."

She spins on her heel and leaves my office. Thankfully, she's used to my mood.

I blow out a breath, undoing my tie completely as I stare out the windows facing downtown Seattle. Clouds hang low over the mountains in the distance. Ferries come and go from the various islands surrounding the city.

It's about as different from where I grew up as it could be.

I've been ignoring the messages for a week now. All from the same attorney from back home in Montana. No.

Not home.

Seattle is home now. The city has been home for the last six years. I've been back a few times since I left, but never stay long. Even if my mom and sister yell at me for it.

I'd rather pay for them to come visit me than go back there.

Tossing my tie onto my desk, I plop down into my black leather chair and drop my elbows onto the heavy wooden desk.

I don't know why someone from back home is wanting

to get in touch with me so badly, but it's not something I can focus on right now.

This acquisition demands my undivided attention.

I've been working on it for months. Coming in early. Staying late. We're in the homestretch. Only a few more hoops to jump through before it can be finalized.

Who knew I had a knack for this kind of stuff? I always enjoyed math in high school, but it wasn't until college that I found out I was *really* good at it. Enough to do something with it for a living.

I bury myself in papers, eating my lunch as I study the numbers to make sure everything is in line for the deal. This is how I made a name for myself here. I can find anything that is out of line on a balance sheet of the company being acquired.

"Mr. Miller?"

Kelly knocks on the door, peeking her head in.

"Is Raven here?"

I glance at the watch on my wrist, seeing I still have thirty minutes before my meeting starts. I know she likes to get here early, but not by this much. Not that I paid attention to how much time had passed since Kelly last came in here.

"There's an attorney here to see you."

"What?"

She looks nervous, chewing her bottom lip. "The one that's been calling you? He says he won't leave until he gets a word with you."

"Fuck," I mutter, scrubbing a hand down my face.

This is not what I need to deal with today. I have too much on my plate. I've borrowed from tomorrow's plate. Hell, even next week's plate.

Being one of the youngest investment bankers at my company doesn't leave a lot of free time. My calendar is scheduled down to the minute. Not a lot of room for unannounced meetings.

"What do you want me to tell him?"

I look down at the stack of papers sitting on my desk. I don't need the interruption right now, but given how persistent he's been, I doubt he'll leave until he's spoken with me.

"Give me five and then send him in."

"Okay, Mr. Miller."

She nods before heading out and shutting the door behind her.

Grabbing my tie from the desk, I loop it around my neck and tighten it. Taking a deep breath, I ready myself for whatever this attorney has to say.

Nervous? I don't get nervous.

I have to be calm, cool, and collected in my line of business. Any sign of weakness, and I'll be taken advantage of.

A knock sounds on the door. Stuffing my hands in my pockets, I turn to see Kelly leading an older man with glasses and a mustache into my office.

"Kade Miller. How are you?" He walks right over to me and extends a hand, which I shake.

"Good. How can I help you today, Mister…"

"Mr. Simms." He adjusts his glasses, dropping into the chair across from my desk and popping open his briefcase. "I'm here regarding the will of Mr. Verne Walters."

"Verne died?"

It's a gut punch. I was home only a few months ago and popped into the ranch to see him. He looked the same as always. I can still picture him with that old Stetson, cigarette hanging from his mouth. His skin was leathery from working out in the sun.

"I'm sorry. Did no one inform you of his passing?"

"No." I scrub a hand down my face. "It's been a busy week and—"

It's why my mom has been calling and texting. She told me to call her as soon as I could. I passed it off as her wanting to catch up, but since I'd only just talked to her, I put it off.

"I'm very sorry for your loss, but it's important I speak with you regarding his will."

"Right."

I smooth a hand down my tie, shifting in my seat.

"Have you heard of The Lost Spur ranch?"

"Yes."

My senses prickle. What in the world is going on?

"He's left it to you." He hands over a sheet of paper.

"What? He left me the ranch?"

"He did. It was all he had left, and with no family remaining, all his possessions are now yours."

"Mine?" I ask. "He never mentioned it."

"The Lost Spur is yours. I should mention there are a few liens on the property that will need to be handled should you keep it, but if you sell—"

"I'm aware of how the process works," I interject. "What do you mean by a few?"

A thick manila envelope is passed over. "Everything is in this file. Profit and loss statements. Current operating costs. Reservations."

"When do I have to make a decision?"

"I'm sorry, a decision?" he asks.

"On what I want to do."

"Mr. Miller. The ranch is yours. There will be some paperwork for you to sign, but once complete, the property and cattle business is yours."

"Is this something I can do here?"

He shakes his head. "I'm afraid not. Due to probate, it will need to be handled in Pinecrest."

Shit.

"When's the soonest this can be done?" I ask.

"Given that I know the county judge, we can get the paperwork done fairly quickly."

"And what then?"

"Then?" He adjust his glasses. "You would be the owner of the ranch."

A ranch in Pinecrest. It sounds like my nightmare.

"Could I sell it?"

"It does require some work."

Of course it couldn't be as easy as signing some paperwork and then selling.

"I have money. Would that help move the process?"

"Mr. Miller." He shifts in his seat. "You cannot throw money at this to make it go away."

Great. And now I sound like a dick.

"I didn't mean it like that."

He stands, looking thoroughly annoyed with me. "I recommend sending all of this over to your attorney and making them aware of what is going on. I'll be in contact with your assistant to let her know the time and place of your meeting. I understand this is a lot, but these things take time."

"Right." I stand, shaking his hand. "Thank you for coming down here to meet with me."

"I wouldn't have had to if you had taken my phone call."

He snaps his briefcase shut before leaving.

Okay then.

I drop down into my chair, the leather squeaking under me.

I inherited a ranch. A place I worked during high

school and during the few summers I came home. Back when I thought…well, that life is gone now.

My life is here.

In what seems like the blink of an eye, my life has changed.

Again.

Chapter Three

KADE

"Are you sure you can manage everything while I'm gone?" I ask, not for the first time.

"Jake is here should anything come up that we need, but it's not like you won't be conferencing in on the calls," Kelly says.

"I don't like being gone in the middle of a merger."

"We're in the homestretch. It'll be fine. Besides, Raven is already looking ahead and buying stock in the Seattle women's soccer team. You'll have something else to worry about soon."

"Of course she is." I laugh. "Call me if you need anything."

"I will. Were you able to pick up the rental?" she asks.

"Headed there now. Thanks for your help with all of this."

"No problem. Call if you need me."

She ends the call and I stuff my phone into my pocket.

My feet take me on the well-known path to the rental car counter. Fake trees and stuffed bears recreate the wildlife you can see in town with portraits of Pinecrest lining the walls. Walking through the airport always feels like I am in a museum.

I never thought I'd be back here so soon after my last visit. When I come to town, it's to see my mom and sister, with the occasional trip to see Verne. That's it. Anything else, and I was at risk of seeing *her*.

I don't know how long I'll be here, but I don't want to see her. I haven't seen her since that night, and I don't plan on starting now. Nerves settle low in my gut at the thought.

I get my SUV from the rental place without issue and head out into the clean, fresh, Montana air. This is one of the things I always miss about being here.

The air.

The cool, crisp fall breeze helps to soothe the uneasy feeling growing inside me.

Getting into the white SUV, I head toward my mom's place. I've made this drive hundreds of times. The mountains and pine trees that line the highway welcome me back. I roll the windows down, letting in the wind.

Damn, does it ever feel good.

Thankfully, I don't have to drive through town to get to Mom's place. With her living on the outskirts, I turn the vehicle down the familiar road. A few people are out on their porches, and it's not a surprise to see my mom waiting for me on her wraparound.

She stands, waving as I pull in.

"Hey, Mom."

"There's my baby boy." She holds her arms out wide for me. Stepping into them, I wrap her in a hug. She smells the same. That clean, laundry scent. "How was your trip?"

I look down at her warm, brown eyes. The same eyes that I have. More gray seems to pepper her short brown bob.

"Fine."

"No trouble?"

"None."

"Your—"

"Hey, Kade!" Grace comes bursting out of the front door.

"Hey, sis."

I pull her in for a hug.

"I didn't think you'd be here for a while longer," she says. "I was planning on going out."

Grace is the spitting image of Mom, including her brown hair and her brown eyes. Hell, we both are.

"Not tonight," Mom chides her. "I have dinner in the crock pot. I figure a good home-cooked meal is exactly what you need."

Stepping inside, the smell of my favorite Mexican casserole greets me. "Oh, man, that smells great, Mom."

She pats me on the stomach as she walks by. "You're too skinny. Are you eating enough out there?"

"Mom," I groan.

"What? I'm allowed to worry. You're my baby boy and you live so far away."

Grace grabs a chip from the bowl resting on the counter and pops it into her mouth. "You'd worry if he lived here."

"At least I can look after you now."

"What do you mean?" I shoot my gaze over to my sister.

"She moved back in after that Kevin dumped her," Mom answers.

"Why did I not hear about this?" I growl.

"Because you never pick up the phone," Grace says.

Heading to the fridge, I grab a beer and crack it open. "I'm busy."

"Too busy for your family?" Mom quirks a brow at me.

"Never."

"Yeah, yeah. At least you're home now," Grace says.

"For how long?" Mom grabs the plates and starts scooping out a heaping portion of dinner for me.

"Unknown," I answer honestly.

"How do you not know?" Grace asks. "Grab me a beer, will ya?"

I nod, grabbing her a drink and taking a seat next to her at the counter.

"It could be a couple of weeks or maybe longer. It just depends on how much work the place needs."

"Do you plan on keeping the ranch?" Mom asks, wiping her hands on a towel and grabbing her own drink.

"What's with all the questions?"

"A mother has to know what is going on with her son."

I snort a laugh before taking a too-hot bite of dinner. So fucking good.

"You know what's going on with me. Busy with work in Seattle and now, owner of The Lost Spur."

"I still can't believe Verne left you the ranch." Grace whistles.

"You and me both."

It's a thought I keep coming back to over the last few days. Trying to get everything sorted out back home before coming here, it was hard to stay focused.

I don't know who is running the ranch now, but wouldn't Verne's right-hand man be better than me, someone who hasn't worked outside in years? I'm more comfortable behind a desk and computer than on a horse.

"Verne always liked you," Mom tells me. "Why wouldn't he leave it to you?"

"Liking someone and leaving them your entire life are two completely different things."

"Well, maybe you'll find out some more information once you sign the paperwork with the lawyers."

"Yeah, maybe."

"Are you going to see anyone while you're here?" Mom asks.

"Besides you two? Who else would I need to see?"

I dig in to my dinner, trying not to worry about how long I'll be here and who I might see. I don't need to worry about that if I keep to the ranch. That should be my only priority while I'm here.

That and making sure my deals back home don't completely fall through.

Kelly is perfectly capable of handling things on my behalf while I work remotely, but I don't want to settle into that pattern here.

I have zero clue what I'm in for when I see the ranch.

"Do you want us to go with you?" Mom asks.

"To meet with the lawyer? No, I'm good."

"I meant the ranch. You know, now that I'm retired, I can help out." She waggles her brows at me. "I watch those design shows. I can help you."

Looking around her house, I know she's done a lot of work to fix things up.

This place wasn't always the greatest growing up, but it was home. Once I started making good money, I sent money home for Mom. It's nice to see that she's been able to work on this place.

New wallpaper and light fixtures. New appliances in the kitchen. It's simple things, but it really looks great.

"Maybe I could use you."

She beams. "I could be your project manager."

"I think that's my job, Mom." I laugh.

"I'm here if you need help."

"Thanks."

"Your sister too."

That earns her a laugh. "I wouldn't trust her with a paintbrush."

"Dick," she calls out.

"What? You know you painted half of the ceiling because you weren't being careful in high school."

"At least I fixed it now." She points a finger in my face.

"Still. I don't know if I need your help." I smirk at her. "We'll see what I'm getting myself into once I get out there."

I'm only hoping I'm not biting off more than I can chew.

Life for me is back in Seattle. It's not in Pinecrest. I'm hoping for a quick transaction and then leaving town.

That's my plan.

I only hope I can stick to it.

Chapter Four

KADE

Dirt billows out from behind the SUV as I drive down the empty road. Scraggly grass lines each side as the mountains loom in the distance.

The Lost Spur gateway greets me. One of the metal spurs hangs haphazardly from one side and rust coats the sign.

Leaning forward to take it in, I pass under it, entering Verne's ranch.

Well, now my ranch. I met with the attorneys today, and after some signatures, the place is mine.

Fences don't look to be in great shape, held together with duct tape and a prayer.

Jesus. I knew the place wasn't looking good, but I didn't think it was this bad. Turning along the drive toward the main building, pine trees rise up on either side of me. I roll the windows down, sucking in a breath of fresh air.

I forgot how good it feels.

A few cars sit in the parking lot, but I bypass them and head toward the barn. I don't know who still works here that I would know, but something I learned from the time I spent here is that the ranch hands always knew what was going on.

I'll start there.

Parking my car, I hop out and slam the door shut behind me. A horse neighs in the pasture ahead of me.

The barn is old. Windows and doors are dusty, with bales of hay stacked along one wall. The sun glares off the high windows from the roof.

Everything looks like it could use a good scrubbing.

The doors are swung wide open and an older man walks out.

"Can I help you?"

"Yeah. I'm Kade Miller. I—"

"The new owner," he interrupts. "Sam Shaw. I'm the lead rancher here. I've been trying to do what I can to keep things running these last few months, but it hasn't been easy."

"What do you mean?" He winces, brown eyes looking at me with curiosity, gauging how much he wants to tell me. "Look, I own the place now, so might as well rip off the Band-Aid."

"The ranch is broke," he says matter-of-factly, running a hand through his graying hair.

"Shit. Really? I haven't had a chance to look at any of the paperwork I got from the lawyers."

"Reservations have been dwindling, and Verne pissed off the main buyer of the cattle, so money hasn't been coming in."

"Fuck," I groan.

Looking around the barn, it seems to be in okay shape. The horses look well fed, at least.

"Verne didn't keep me updated on the finances, but I knew what was going on. I've done what I can, but I don't know how much longer we can keep going without an influx of cash."

"Well, that I do have, fortunately."

Or unfortunately as I grab a board and it pops right off the stall.

"We've got a good program in place for horse training, but we haven't been able to bring people in. No marketing equals no guests."

"You any good at that?" I ask, eyeing him.

He waggles his head back and forth. "Some experience, back in my college days."

I smile at him. "When was that? Back before electricity was invented."

"Fuck off, kid." He laughs. "I'm forty-five. I'm not ancient."

"Then you might have to start doing what you can to bring people in. Care to show me the main building?"

"You sure?" He cocks a brow at me. "It's nothing fancy."

"Gotta start somewhere."

I follow him on the well-worn trail from the barn to the guesthouse. A few paths branch out from the main one, leading off to the guest cabins. I have no idea what state they're in.

A small, hand-painted sign, surrounded by wildflowers, welcomes people inside.

"Still have this here, I see." I pat it as we walk by.

Sam smiles back at me. "Verne could never part with it. Not when his Arlene made it for him."

I give him a sad smile. "Hopefully they're together."

"I'm sure they are." He claps me on the back as he holds open the door for me. "No doubt she's yelling at him for smoking his cigarettes."

That pulls a laugh from me. "God, I forgot how much she used to yell at him for that."

"They were quite the pair, weren't they?"

A musty smell wafts over me as we walk inside. Looking around, I take it all in. Wallpaper peels from the old plaster in the corner. Cobwebs cling to the ceiling. The carpet beneath me is frayed.

"Reenie. What are you doing up here?" Sam comes to an abrupt stop. "Where's Joey?"

Joey? The same Joey that used to be best friends with… never mind. That's not my concern right now.

Right now, this dilapidated ranch is.

"It's three. She had to go pick Max up from school and drop him off at her parents'."

He nods. "Right. Then I guess I'm introducing you to the new owner."

"Owner?" She straightens. The woman, likely the same age as my mom, gives me a warm smile as she sticks her hand out. "I've been waiting to see who comes in and takes over."

"Kade Miller."

"Reenie Jones. I only started working at the ranch a few months ago."

I gaze around the lobby. "I used to work on the ranch in high school. It's been a while since I've been here."

"And now you're the owner?"

"Yup." I nod.

"What do you plan on doing with the place?" she asks.

Isn't that the million-dollar question?

"I've got some time to figure it out." I brush my hand over the faded wallpaper. "Looks like it needs a lot of work."

If I have any hope of selling the place, it looks like I'm

going to have to be here to help. Which means staying longer than I planned.

An old computer blinks while a large calendar sits open—with no reservations for the next week, it seems.

"Then I guess we have our work cut out for us," Sam says.

"Look, I know you don't know me, but I could use your help fixing this place up. It won't be easy, and you might think I'm some city boy who's not used to hard work."

He laughs, crossing his arms over his chest. Arms that show they don't mind doing what's necessary to keep things going.

"I know you from what Verne told me. That old bastard loved you, so that means you're good stock. I'll do whatever I can to help you. Even if you decide you don't want anything to do with this place."

"Thanks." I stick out my hand for him to shake. "I appreciate it."

"When do you want to get started?"

"How about Monday? Take the weekend and then dive in."

"Sounds good. I can talk to the other guys, get them on board."

"Perfect. Who's the manager up front? I'd like to talk to them Monday."

Sam shakes his head. "We don't have one. They quit when Verne died. Joey's been managing things for now."

"Great," I jest. "So on top of everything else, I need to hire someone."

"Joey's good. Just a lot going on with her kid."

I massage the muscle in my neck, tension growing there. The list of what needs done here seems to be never-ending.

"We'll see." My stomach growls. "I'm going to head into town and grab something to eat. Here's my number. Text me a list of everything you need done in the barn."

"Anything?" he asks, taking my card from me.

"Anything. I'm going to sort everything out and see what all needs done and prioritize from there."

"Got it. Thanks, Kade."

"See you Monday, Sam."

Heading back out to my SUV, dirt sticks to my leather shoes. Definitely something I can't wear again out here. I'll need to see if I still have my old boots. They might be buried in my closet at my mom's place.

I'll also need to figure out where the fuck I'm going to stay. The smart option would be to stay here on the ranch so I can save the money on a rental. Mom offered me to stay with her, but I don't know if I could manage that for more than a few days. Especially with my sister being between jobs—and relationships—and crashing there as well.

No.

As I head back into town, I decide the ranch is the best place to be. I'll figure out what I need and get it sorted before Sam and I start the hard work of fixing everything up. At least he's on board. If he can get the other ranch hands to help, that's one item off my list.

Passing by the Hash 'N Hop, I decide a greasy burger is what I need right now. Tearing off my tie, I toss it into the front seat as I head inside. Shouldering open the door, the smell of grease assaults my senses.

Just like it used to.

The place is packed to the brim with people. There's one lone stool open at the bar next to a little girl with blonde pigtails.

"This seat taken?"

"No." She looks up from the picture she's coloring. "But I shouldn't tell you that."

"Why not?"

I grab a plastic menu and take a quick glance, not really needing it since I know what I'm getting.

"I'm not supposed to talk to strangers."

"My name is Kade. What's yours?"

"Poppy."

"And who's that?" I nod to a stuffed goose sitting next to her.

"Strawberry."

There's something familiar about her. About the animal sitting by her. I can't pinpoint what.

It's not like I see a lot of people when I come to town. Mom, Grace, and Verne. And it's not like I can see one of them anymore.

The server comes over and takes my order, getting me a Coke and setting it in front of me. I take a long, refreshing drink. Just what I needed.

"You should get a milkshake," Poppy tells me.

"Oh yeah?" I eye her. "What's the best flavor?"

"Chocolate."

"Not strawberry?"

She shakes her head. "Strawberry can't have strawberries."

I smile. "Why not?"

"Because she's a strawberry. Duh."

"Poppy," a voice hisses behind us. "What have I told you about talking to strangers?"

That voice.

I haven't heard that voice in six long years. Since the night I left town and never looked back.

That's why this little girl looks familiar.

Spinning on my stool, my gaze lands on her, standing in a pink shirt with her blonde hair tied up in a bandanna. She looks the exact same.

Presley King.

The woman that broke my heart.

Chapter Five

PRESLEY

"Poppy. What have I told you about talking to strangers?" I chide, rounding the counter with plates balanced on my arms.

Poppy is the most outgoing person. I don't know where she gets it from. All of her teachers say she's the most talkative in class, sometimes to her detriment.

Trying to teach her about stranger danger? It's hard.

"I'm not, mama." She says it like it's the most obvious thing in the world. "He asked about Strawberry. I told him I can't talk to strangers and he said his name was Kade."

"Kade?"

I haven't heard that name in years. Haven't thought about it in months. Okay, so that's a lie—I think about it daily, but I try not to.

There is no possible way that it's *that* Kade she's talking to. It's a common name, right?

My gaze moves to the man sitting next to her and I'd recognize that physique anywhere.

Kade Miller.

The man who left town and shattered me. Every nerve

is tingling as a hard stare faces me. I map his features. The harder jaw line. Longer hair. Closed-off brown eyes. Strong hands and biceps. Everything about this person is Kade. *My* Kade. And yet, he's an entirely different person.

He's sitting on the stool next to Poppy, and it makes my heart clatter around in my chest.

Our eyes are locked on one another, neither of us moving.

When was the last time I saw him? The week he left town? I know he's come back over the years, but I've never seen him. I heard the whispers. I didn't need to see him. Didn't need the complication of him in my life.

I had my daughter to worry about.

Kade stands, but doesn't say a word as he turns to leave the diner. I'm still holding my breath, staring into the space he vacated.

"Oh my God."

"Excuse me, can we have our order?" a voice calls out, stirring me into action.

I set the plates down, wiping my hands before heading to where Poppy is.

"Poppy. You can't talk to strangers," I scold her.

"But—"

"No buts. Now, finish your milkshake and we'll go home in a few minutes."

Thank God it's the end of my shift because I don't know if I could focus right now.

"Are you okay? You look like you've seen a ghost," Rylee says.

"Kade is here."

"What?" She gasps, looking over my shoulder.

"I mean, he was. He was talking to Poppy."

"You're kidding."

I shake my head. "What's he doing in town?"

"I don't know. I haven't heard anything. Do you think it has anything to do with Verne passing away?"

"Maybe." I blow out a breath. "God, I completely snapped at Poppy."

"Do you think Poppy knows?" Rylee asks.

"She wouldn't have a clue," I say.

Rylee holds out her hand. "I'll cover your tables. Take Poppy home."

"Are you sure?"

"Yes." Then her eyes go wide. "Do you think it has anything to do with what Serena said?"

"What? What did she say?"

"About your reading she did."

"The lovers? I doubt it." I snort. That's the last thing I need to be thinking about. "Look, I'll see you tomorrow, okay?"

She nods. "Text us if you need anything, okay?"

"I will. Thanks."

Heading to the locker room in the back of the kitchen, I take off my apron and hang it up.

Kade Miller is in town. He was *here*.

I sling my bag over my shoulder and walk out to take Poppy's hand to walk home.

"I'm sorry, Mom," she says, looking up at me.

"It's okay. I didn't mean to snap at you. But if I'm not there, I don't want you talking to strangers, okay?"

"Okay." She nods.

We're both quiet on the walk home.

I have enough going on in my life other than to worry about my ex coming back into our lives. Sneaking a peek at Poppy, it brings back up all the feelings when I first found out I was pregnant.

After Kade left, I was inconsolable. My life changed in the blink of an eye. Kade was gone and I found myself engaged to Paul. All because of my dad. The only thing that got me through was finding out I was pregnant.

It wasn't until Poppy that I was able to pull myself together. I had to. I couldn't fall apart if I had a baby.

Everything I do is for Poppy. It always has been.

But why is Kade here? Will he be back at the diner? I doubt it, considering he knows I work there now. I don't know how long the two of us were locked in a stare down, but it felt like forever.

Now I'm going to worry about running into him around town. Can I handle seeing him again?

I guess we'll see. I've done a lot harder things in my life. Seeing Kade again? It's not something I thought I could handle, but I survived.

I've been in survival mode these last few months. I'm tired. Tired of it and ready to get my life back. So what's another curveball of having my ex here?

Just one more thing to survive. I can do it, right?

Chapter Six

KADE

Staring at myself in the mirror, I give myself one last pep talk.

"You can do this. You've done a lot harder things."

Yeah, like bumping into Presley for the first time after six years. Not like I talked to her, but what would I have said?

Nice to see you again?

How have you been?

What's been going on with you the last few years?

She had a kid.

Presley has a daughter. One that is the spitting image of her. That's something I'm still not over. Once I figured out the connection, I couldn't stay there.

She moved on with her life. I guess I was the only one holding a torch. Not that I didn't try to move on, but no relationship ever stuck. I was more scarred than I thought from Presley getting engaged to another man.

That's the last thing I need to be worried about today.

Today? I'm meeting the staff here at the ranch.

Whether I keep this place or not, it's going to affect all of these people. The very least I can do is talk to them.

I have no idea how it's going to go over. I don't know who works here. What if they only see an outsider, even though I was born and raised here?

Fuck.

I really need to stop letting my train of thought run away.

Grabbing my phone, I stuff it in my pocket and head down to the lobby with a few minutes to spare. I stop on the stairs to see everyone is already gathered.

That's a good sign. At least I won't have to wait on anyone.

When my foot hits the bottom step, all eyes turn to me and the chatter stops immediately.

"Hi, everyone."

All eyes are fixed on me, but it doesn't bother me. Merger meetings are way harder than this.

"What are you going to do with the place?"

I don't have to worry about beating around the bush with that one.

"Right now? We're going to get this place fixed up. After that, we'll see."

"Are we going to have jobs?" someone else calls out from the back.

"For the time being, yes. I want to keep things running as normally as possible. I know we have a few guests for the next couple of weeks, but hopefully we can increase revenue streams."

"Do you even know our revenue?"

I don't miss the bitterness in whoever's voice this is.

I scrub a hand down my face. "I only got to town last week. I've got a lot to learn about the ranch, so I'm counting on all of you to help me out."

A scoff.

I have my work cut out for me.

"I know I might seem like an outsider, but trust me, I know this ranch. I worked with Verne in high school here back when it was the place to be, and that's my goal. To bring it back to what it used to be."

Sam stands tall in the back, with Joey and Reenie flanking his sides, giving me a confident nod.

"I'll be meeting with everyone today to get an idea of what you do here and see how I can help you do your job. Until then, business as usual."

Looking around, I spot some unfamiliar faces. Maybe dealing with them will be easier before talking to Joey. I point at Sam and head back to my office.

It's not the tidiest of spaces, but that can come later. Papers are bursting out of the filing cabinet. I can't decide if I want to trash them all or spend the time going through them.

Considering this space used to be Verne's, it's hard to want to get rid of anything, even the worn frames hanging crooked on the walls. Something about changing this feels like I'm erasing him.

"That seemed to go well."

The door shuts and Sam drops into a rickety chair across from the old, wooden desk. It's the only solid thing in this room.

I shrug a shoulder and sit in the black, dusty office chair. "Definitely could have gone worse."

"If it helps, I talked to all the guys this morning and they're on board. They like their jobs, so if they can help and stick around longer, they'll do what they can."

"Thanks. I have a feeling not everyone is going to be that amenable."

"Really?" Sam asks, pulling off his cowboy hat and resting it on his knee. "Why do you think that?"

I think back to the two faces in that crowd of people that are going to cause me grief.

"I have a history with a few people here."

"What kind of history?" Sam asks.

"We knew each other back in high school."

"Did you dump them?" He guffaws.

I shake my head. "Nothing like that. But I haven't seen them in a few years and I don't want them to hinder my plans."

"You tell me if anyone tries anything and I'll be sure to talk to them."

I study the older man in front of me. He has the air about him that people trust him. That he's a leader around here. If there's anyone that I think I'll be able to count on, it's him.

"You ever think about doing more than just working in the barn?"

He shakes his head. "Can't say that I have. Verne was a stubborn ass."

"You got that right. Never let anyone help him with anything."

"Probably why he let this place get away from him." Sam looks around. "You need anything from me? Or do you want me to send in the next victim?"

I wince. "Do they really think it's going to be that bad?"

"No. I'm giving you grief, kid."

"Seriously, I'm not that much younger than you."

He pops his hat back on his head. "Still young enough to be my kid. I'll see you later, boss."

I cross Sam off the list of people I've spoken to. My goal is to make it through everyone on the ranch today so I can hopefully get out and go for a ride. It's something I haven't done in years.

Back when I used to work here, I loved taking Lady out for a ride. Roaming the acres of land with her was fun.

But before I can do that, there's a knock on the door.

"Come in."

The person who waltzes inside has a no bullshit look about her. One that I haven't seen in years.

"Kade Miller."

"Georgia Halliwell."

She crosses her arms over her chest, leaning back in the chair. Her face says don't mess with her *or* her best friend.

Her blonde hair is pulled into a low bun, and she wears a red plaid shirt with jeans and boots. A name tag is pinned to the front of her shirt.

"So, *Georgia*. What is it that you do here?"

"After all these years, that's what you lead with?" She scoffs.

"Considering it's my job, yes."

It's not like I have any beef with her. More so her best friend.

"Unbelievable. You come back after all these years like nothing happened." She shakes her head, muttering to herself.

"Like nothing happened? Believe me, I'm well aware of what *happened* all those years ago."

Fire blazes in her blue eyes as she narrows her gaze on me. She's already written me off after what I did all those years ago.

And yet, she doesn't have the first clue on what happened.

"You mean breaking my best friend's heart?"

"Not how I remember it," I snap.

Fuck. I shove a hand through my hair. This is the last thing I want to be talking to her about.

In and out. Some time to fix this place up and sell it to someone that will hopefully agree to keep the staff and the ranch.

Conversations with Presley's best friend? Not what I want to be dealing with.

"Yes, leaving her high and dry makes you the good person in this scenario." She rolls her eyes at me.

"Are you going to make this harder than it is? Because if you don't want to be here, I can find someone else to do…whatever it is you do."

I don't want to have any conversations about Presley or her daughter. Seeing them once was hard enough. The evidence that she moved on without me?

Yeah, I don't need to have it thrown in my face on a daily basis.

"I'm a horse trainer. I work under Sam."

"And Joey works here too."

"Observant."

"You do realize I'm your boss now, right?"

"Doesn't mean you didn't hurt my best friend and I'm pissed as hell about it."

"Is that what you think?" I scoff.

"It's what I know to be true."

The look Georgia throws my way tells me she's ready to castrate me. Probably the same look Joey gave me too.

I'm surprised one of them hasn't already done it. In high school, wherever Presley was, Georgia wasn't far behind. The two of them were as thick as thieves and it seems nothing has changed.

Me?

I cut all ties with Pinecrest. It was easier to move on that way.

"Anything else you want to know?" Georgia asks, not as defensive as before.

"Look. I know you hate me. I can't say you're my favorite person either, but we're both going to be working here. I'll stay out of your way if you stay out of mine. I can talk to Sam if I need anything. And as long as the guests are happy, I'm happy."

"Good." She nods.

I return her nod. "You're free to go."

She doesn't say another word as she leaves the office, closing the door behind her.

Fuck. I have a headache and I've talked to two people. I have no idea what the rest of the day is going to hold, but I have a feeling a lot of my days are going to be like this in the coming weeks.

People are resistant to change. It's the one thing I know about life. I hate change. The people at my firm in Seattle hate change. With most mergers ending in lost jobs, no one likes it.

Here? I'm hoping to get everyone on board to get this place into shape. I hope more people are like Sam and not Georgia.

Not that I don't think she'll help, but damn, I don't want to deal with people hating me on reputation alone.

It's not like I wanted to leave.

I had my entire life here mapped out. A white house with a wraparound porch and a swing. Two, maybe three kids.

A good life.

That all went out the window in one night.

The thought of settling down here again makes it feel like the walls are closing in. I can fix this place up and go back to Seattle. My life isn't here anymore. It's in the city.

I can sell this place then get the fuck out of Pinecrest. Should be easy enough, right?

Chapter Seven

PRESLEY

"Why are they always out of the good kind?" Poppy whines.

I shake my head. "I don't know, baby. Are you sure you don't want the yellow box?"

Her nose turns up in disgust. "It's too cheesy."

"Then we can't have mac and cheese for dinner tonight."

"Why can't Mr. Moore get me the blue kind?"

I smile down at her. "Even for his favorite customer, I don't think he can."

"Can we have pizza then?"

"No. We can't have pizza. How about I make chicken and corn for us?"

I get the same look. Disgust. "I don't like corn. It's too crunchy."

"Grilled cheese?"

Another shake of her head. "You burned it last time."

"That was one time," I scoff. "You like grilled cheese."

"Do we have ketchup in case you burn it?"

"Yes. We have ketchup."

"Fine. But can I have chips with it too?"

"Sure. Let's get more bread."

Steering the cart, we leave the pasta aisle and head to the bread and come to a dead stop.

Kade.

Shit. There he is, standing at the end of the aisle. Unassuming in a white T-shirt, jeans, and a pair of cowboy boots. I know Pinecrest is a small town, but why do I keep running into him?

He spots us, and before he can turn and run, Poppy pipes up. "Can I go say hi to him, Mom?"

What am I supposed to say to her? He's a stranger? She can't talk to him because I don't know what to say to him?

I give a small nod and she goes running up to him.

"Hi, Kade."

He kneels down to her level. "Hi, Poppy. What are you up to?"

"Shopping with Mom."

"Oh, yeah? Getting anything good?"

"They don't have the macaroni I like."

"That's too bad."

"Mom is going to make us grilled cheese."

"Do you like it with ketchup?" he asks. "I like it with ketchup, but people think that's gross."

"I love it with ketchup!" Poppy beams at him. "Especially when Mom burns it."

"Hey! I burned it once."

"It was yucky," Poppy whispers out of the corner of her mouth.

Kade's eyes flit between the two of us, like he's studying us.

"Ketchup always helps," he finally says, steeling his face before standing. He nods in my direction. "Presley."

"Kade."

My voice is soft, still not sure how to interact with him.

"Enjoy your night." He tips his head before walking down the aisle and leaving.

"He's nice," Poppy says, grabbing a corner of the cart and pulling it after her.

"Yeah."

It's still weird seeing her interact with Kade.

Her *father*.

Now that he's in town, he deserves to know. Needs to know. He left town and I had no way of getting ahold of him. Even his mom and sister shut me out. When Poppy came along, everyone thought she was Paul's, and I went with it. No sense in saying anything when Kade was gone and never coming back.

The man can barely stand to look at me, so how in the world am I going to tell him that Poppy is his?

Pulling out my phone, I text the girls.

PRESLEY

> Any chance you guys are free to come over tonight for dinner and wine?

JOEY

> I am. My parents have Max for a sleepover

RYLEE

> Me too

GEORGIA

> Same

GEORGIA

> Everything okay?

> I need to talk about Kade

> **JOEY**
> I've been waiting for this

> We bumped into him at the store

> **RYLEE**
> How awkward was that?

> I'll tell you over grilled cheese

> **JOEY**
> I'll bring the wine

> **GEORGIA**
> I have a feeling we might need vodka for this

> Yeah…

> **RYLEE**
> We'll meet you at your place

"YOUR AUNTS ARE GOING to come over for dinner tonight," I tell Poppy.

"But it's a school night," she says matter-of-factly.

"It's okay. Moms are allowed to have people over on school nights." I wink at her.

Grabbing our favorite cookies, I load up on the rest of the essentials for the week. Nothing fancy since Poppy is so picky, but by the time we check out and head home, the girls are already there.

"Hey, Pop," Rylee calls out.

Poppy goes running to her, her bag with the bread bumping against her leg. "Hi, Aunt Rylee."

She gets scooped up into a big hug as I follow them up the stairs.

"You doing okay?" Georgia asks.

"Not really."

I haven't been okay for a while now. Since I walked out on my husband. Since my dad died.

And the worst of it? Seeing Kade come back and look at me like I'm a stranger.

It's a knife to the heart.

Digging out my keys, I unlock the door to our tiny apartment and shoulder it open. A far cry from the house I shared with Paul, but it's mine.

Paintings of Poppy's paper the drab, beige walls. An old couch I picked up on sale takes up most of the living room, and a kitchen table sits right behind it. The kitchen is small with old appliances, with a cut out window that lets me watch Poppy while cooking.

Now, it's Joey and Poppy emptying the groceries as Rylee pushes me into a chair.

"What's for dinner?" Joey asks Poppy as the two of them start to unpack the groceries.

"Grilled cheese."

"Want me to help?" she asks. "I'm really good at grilled cheese."

"Yes." Poppy grins at her before giggling. "Mom burns it."

"Stop calling me out, Poppy!" I say, injecting a lightness to my voice that I don't feel.

"I'll pour us some wine," Rylee says.

"Make mine a big glass," I say, shaking my head. "I still can't believe he inherited the ranch."

After hearing the news from Georgia and Joey, my jaw dropped. I shouldn't have been surprised. Verne loved Kade. He was always there for him, helping out after school and during the summer while he was home on break from college.

Rylee brings the bottle and four glasses to the table, pouring me a healthy serving. I don't waste a second and drink down a gulp.

"People seem to like him," Georgia says.

"He's a likable guy," I reply. "We all liked him."

"Yeah, some of us even loved him," Rylee whispers.

"Who are you talking about?" Poppy asks, head bobbing above the counter.

"No one you know," I say.

She shrugs a shoulder and goes back to helping Joey.

"How am I supposed to tell Kade that he's...well, you know?"

I mouth *her dad* when Poppy isn't looking.

"In your defense," Joey starts, "he left and never came back."

"But now that he's back, how do I even start that conversation?"

These girls are the only ones that know Poppy is Kade's. Well, them and Paul. But to Paul's credit, he took care of Poppy like she was his. For the most part.

"Do you think he knows?" Georgia asks.

"How would he?" I ask. "She looks just like me."

"Here's your sandwich." Poppy brings a plate with a sandwich, cut diagonally down the middle, with a blob of ketchup next to it.

"Thanks, baby." I kiss her head as she goes back into the kitchen. "You're a good chef."

"Aunt Joey knows what she's doing."

Being a single mom, if she didn't cook, she'd spend all her money on eating out. Not what you want to do with a three-year-old at home. At least Max is less picky than Poppy.

"Maybe you can come out to the ranch one day and

talk to him," Georgia suggests, pulling my attention back to the matter at hand.

"Might be kind of hard when he's said one word to me since coming back."

"Want me to handcuff him to his desk?" Georgia laughs. "That'll get him to listen."

I roll my eyes, taking another sip of wine. "Not exactly how I plan on that conversation going."

"But it would mean you get to talk to him," Rylee says. "He can't run out on you if he's locked up."

"Mom, can I watch a movie during dinner?" Poppy asks.

"Sure."

So much for limiting TV time today.

But my thoughts are too scrambled to worry about it as she settles into her spot on the couch and fires up the screen for her favorite.

I dig into my own dinner. Damn, Joey really does make a good grilled cheese.

The background noise of the movie lets us have our own conversation. I voice my biggest worry.

"What if Kade hates me and he takes it out on Poppy?"

"Do you really think he would do that?" Joey asks, tying her dark hair up before tearing a bite off her sandwich.

I shrug a shoulder. "I don't know. Kade isn't the same person as he was."

I know nothing about his life. All I know is he took over the ranch and that's it. Hell, he knows nothing about my life. Well, except for the fact that I have Poppy and work at the diner.

"Kade wouldn't do that. If he has any ounce of love

for you—at any point in his life—he wouldn't hurt you by hurting Poppy," Georgia says.

I blow out a breath. "Maybe the next time I see him, I can talk to him and see if we can set a time to have another talk."

"A talk to talk," Joey snickers. "Easy."

Easy.

I hope it'll be easy. Because nothing about Kade these last few days has been easy, from seeing him to talking with him at the store. I didn't realize that when he left, I built a wall up around my heart to keep him out.

Will I be able to keep him out? Better yet, will I be able to keep my heart intact?

I survived Kade leaving once. I don't know if I can do it again.

Chapter Eight

KADE

Crack.

Another swing. Another hole in the side of the barn that needs to be torn down and replaced.

If we plan on having cattle here, we need this to be in tip-top shape. Not the run-down mess that Verne let the old barn turn into.

It needs to be torn down to the studs and rebuilt, but I know that is going to get expensive. If I can help with the demo, it'll be somewhat cheaper.

Not to mention it's free therapy.

Because I can't get the image of Presley and her daughter out of my mind. It's been haunting me since the minute I left the old general store.

Some things really haven't changed around here. Mr. Moore's store is still the same as it was in high school. Old wooden aisles half filled with food. Most people go to the shinier, newer store outside of town, but those that have lived in Pinecrest their whole lives? They still go there.

Which is how I ended up running into Presley again.

With her daughter.

Poppy.

When Presley and I were together in high school, we always talked about what our kids would look like.

Who would they look like? Me or her? Who would they act like? What would their personalities be?

"Mini-Presleys," I always said.

If that isn't the truth now…

Poppy is a mirror to her mother. But there's something that is still niggling the back of my brain.

The way her mouth quirked at the side when she whispered.

Something I've always done.

There's no way Poppy is mine. Presley would have told me. There's no way she wouldn't have.

Except…I left without a second look back. Left my phone and picked up a new one in Seattle. I didn't want anything tying me to my life here.

Another hit to the wall and wood goes flying. Dust blows back, hitting me in the face. Wiping the sweat from my brow, I drop down onto the bale of hay to give my arms a rest.

Nothing like working out in the barn to work out my anger.

"You got something against the barn?" Sam asks, nodding his head toward the hole in the wall.

Pulling my hat off my head, I toss it down next to me. "Sorry. Just working some things out."

"Anything I can help with?" he asks.

"How much do you now about Presley King?" I ask.

"Presley? I know she's friends with Joey and Georgia, but not much else." He grins down at me from where he stands. "I don't know if you know this, but I'm a bit older than your crowd."

That pulls a laugh from me. "You're not that old. Not the way you're helping renovate this place."

"You're too kind." He claps me on the shoulder. "Why are you asking about Presley?"

"Curious, is all. Do you know how old her daughter is?"

"Poppy?" Sam rolls his eyes back and forth, like he's trying to think it through. "Five? Six, maybe? Not quite sure."

Fuck.

I'm not around kids enough to know how old they are. I was hoping she might be younger than that. There'd be no question she was Paul's.

My jaw grinds together just thinking that name.

Fucking Paul.

The right guy from the right side of town. Someone suitable for the precious King family line.

Me?

Presley's parents hated me from the minute I picked her up for our first date in an old tan car that I borrowed from Verne. Something he loaned me until I saved enough to get my own ride.

"You okay? You look like you're ready to punch a wall."

I scrub a hand down my face. "Yeah. I'm trying to figure a few things out."

"I'd ask if you want help, but you seem to have things taken care of in here."

Looking behind me, the wall is almost completely gone. "Damn. Maybe I should try to work more things out in here."

"You should. Reenie doesn't want anyone's help at the lodge."

I nod. "When I asked if I could give my input on the wallpaper, she told me unless I chopped my dick off, I get no say."

"Damn. Don't get in her way."

"I have to give her credit though. She's got a good eye. What she's already done looks great."

Sam gives me a concerned look. "Are you sure you want to be living in a construction zone?"

I wave him off. "I'm good. There's worse places I could be. Besides, you can't beat the commute."

"You got that right. I've got to head back to pick up the guests for their trail ride."

"We have guests?" I ask.

"We do. Joey says we have a few more reservations the week after too."

"Good."

More guests means more money. I'm pouring everything I have into this place to fix it up, but I need every last penny.

Because fixing up an entire ranch is more than I thought it would be.

"Don't go breaking anything while you're trying to fix this place up. We don't need you knocking the entire thing down."

I flip him off as he gives me a shit-eating grin. "I don't plan on it."

"Good. I'll see you around."

He's off, leaving me alone again with my thoughts.

That inevitably circle back around to Presley.

Fuck. I can't get her out of my mind. Is this what it's going to be like every day? Me stressing about seeing her? Seeing her daughter?

Hell, maybe even *my* daughter?

Fuck it. I can't keep doing this.

I need to talk to her. No matter how badly it hurts to see Presley, I have to have a conversation with her.

Grabbing my keys, I head to my truck.

Because this can't wait a minute longer.

Chapter Nine

PRESLEY

Finally. *Finally.* The last person leaves the diner, ending what feels like the longest shift ever. My feet are aching and the burn mark etched into my forearm still throbs.

All because I was too busy thinking about Kade.

Damn him.

I don't want to be thinking about him. But I can't stop. He's consumed my every waking thought since the minute he showed up at the diner. Hell, he's even showing up in my dreams.

That Kade is mean. Yelling at me for making him leave town and not telling him about Poppy, then turning her against me before the two of them move to Mars.

Not that I have to worry about them moving to Mars, but at least real-life Kade is nicer than dream Kade.

I drop down onto one of the bar stools, catching my head in my hands.

"You want some help closing up?" Rylee yells from the kitchen. Betty's already left, leaving the two of us here on our own.

"I'm good. I just need a minute."

"You sure?"

Looking up, I wave her off. "Go hang out with Chase. At least one of us can have a life tonight."

She winks back at me. "I owe you one."

"Yeah, yeah."

The sounds of her dropping things in her locker filter through to the bar before I hear her lock the back door as she leaves.

The overhead lights turn off—set to a timer—casting everything in pink and blue hues. It's quiet. Silent.

It's one of the few times where it's just me and I can catch my breath. With Poppy at the babysitter for another hour or so, I can take my time going through the motions of closing the diner.

Wiping down the tables one last time. Counting the register. Making sure the dishwashers are running before the morning rush.

The overhead door chimes as I count the last of the quarters.

Fuck.

I completely forgot to lock the door. That's not like me. Not that it's unsafe in Pinecrest, but you can never be too careful.

"Sorry, we're—"

I can't finish because standing in front of me is Kade.

An angry Kade.

A white, short-sleeved button-up is cuffed over his biceps. Jeans stretch across his thick thighs. And that cowboy hat?

I hate that it has butterflies exploding in my stomach. It's the first time the two of us have been alone since he got back. Nerves jangle my body.

"Is she mine?"

It's barely more than a whisper, but I feel the weight of his words like an anvil on my chest.

"Yes."

His jaw ticks as his eyes narrow at me. He opens his mouth to speak, but stops. Anger radiates off him in waves.

"Why didn't you tell me? Don't you think I deserved to know that I've had a daughter for the last five years?" He seethes. "Fuck, Pres."

That snaps me into action. "How the hell was I supposed to tell you, Kade? Hmm? That Poppy is your daughter? *You* left town. *You* changed your number. *You* didn't look back. You're the one that threw me away."

"Me?" He growls, taking a step toward me. "One second you and I are planning our future and then the next, you're engaged. What the fuck was I supposed to do, Presley? Did you ever think about that?"

"You think I wanted Paul? You broke my heart, Kade. I was a wreck."

"What, and I was out running around like I was on top of the world? I felt like the trash you threw away."

"Fuck you, Kade." My voice wobbles. "You knew how I felt about you."

"Did I?"

"You didn't fight for me. You didn't fight for *us*."

"Do you really think your dad would have allowed it?"

"He didn't get a say over my life," I fire back.

"That's news to me," he scoffs.

I stab a finger at his chest. "I guess we'll never know, will we?"

He grabs my hand, holding it at his chest. His brown eyes are alive with emotion. All the same ones that are swimming through me.

Frustration.

Resentment.

Fire.

Want.

The tension in the diner is a live wire. One spark, and the entire building is going to go up in flames. One second. Two. In the blink of an eye, Kade is moving, crushing his mouth against mine.

It takes a beat for my brain to catch up to what's happening, but not my body. My fingers dig into his shoulders to pull him closer.

Every nerve in my body is alight as his tongue demands entry. I grant it, getting my first taste of Kade in years.

Oh God. I haven't felt anything this good in years. Since he left. The scruff on his jaw amps up my need as he tips my chin up to change the angle.

He slows his move. Savoring, as if he's relearning what makes me sing. What I like. He tugs my bottom lip between his teeth before licking away the sting.

"Kade." My voice drips with need.

He trails a path of kisses along my jaw to suck my earlobe into his mouth. I purr. Heat travels through my veins as I move my hands up and down his back.

Kade lifts me into his arms, setting me down on the barstool. I link my feet behind him to pull him closer. To feel every inch of him against me. The broad muscles of his chest. His strong hands as they squeeze my ass.

Every. Single. Inch. Of. Him.

"Do you know how much you drive me crazy?" Kade growls, nipping at my neck. "How much I wish I didn't want you, Pres?"

I rock into him, feeling his hard dick against my center.

"I wish I didn't want you either."

It's a lie. Perhaps the biggest lie I've ever told myself.

All I want is Kade Miller. I want him more than anything in the world.

He smiles against my neck. "Good."

This time, when he moves back to my mouth, his touch is soft. He alternates between featherlight touches and nibbling on my bottom lip.

"You know just what I like." I toss my head back as he sucks on my pulse. "So good, Bubs."

It's a bucket of ice water thrown over us. The moment passes and is over in the blink of an eye. Kade steps back, wiping his mouth as he stares down at me.

Shit. The old nickname slipped out. It felt like I was back in high school, the two of us making out in the back of his car. It was like nothing had changed—no years, no distance, no time apart.

"I have to go."

He leaves in a flash.

Kade is gone.

Again.

Leaving me to clean up the pieces.

Chapter Ten

PRESLEY

"Hey, Pres. You want to do me a favor?" Betty calls out, flipping a large stack of hash browns on the grill.

"Sure. What's up?"

"I've got a delivery order. Think you could manage it?"

"Sure. Where's it going?"

She smiles at me. A knowing smile that has an unease settling in my gut. Why do I have a feeling I know where this is going?

"The Lost Spur."

Of course.

"Okay."

"Think you can manage that?"

Betty flips the food into a Styrofoam to-go container and closes the lid.

"Why couldn't I?"

"I don't know. A certain hunk out there that seems to be keeping you on your toes?"

"What do you mean?"

She waggles her brows at me. "Mr. Moore was telling

everyone about you running into each other the other day at the general store."

I love Pinecrest. I never want to leave. It's my home—my favorite place in the world. But damn it, there are some days I hate it. Can no one keep their nose out of other people's business?

"We ran into each other. Nothing dramatic happened."

"Really? You run into the love of your life and *nothing* happened?" Betty exclaims. "I don't believe you."

"We can be civil adults." I brush a loose lock of hair out of my face. "Now, do you want me to deliver the order or not?" I give her a fake smile. One that she can totally read based on her reaction. "I'm a big girl. I can handle it."

"Good." She nods behind her. "Everything is almost ready to go. Just need to finish the hash browns."

"It's nice you're making them breakfast," I say, starting to pack everything into boxes to make it easier to carry.

"You think I'm doing this for free? Kade called me this morning requesting food. I'm happy to oblige for any paying customer." She snorts at me. "Now, make sure to get a good tip for me."

She winks at me as I shoulder open the back door to the delivery van.

It doesn't take much to amp up my nerves as Betty comes outside to pass over the last bit of food. I haven't been able to stop thinking about Kade since the other night.

Since he attacked my mouth with his.

I wish I could say it didn't affect me, but it did. It rearranged every cell in my body.

When Kade left all those years ago, I was able to put him behind me. *Eventually.*

I tried to make things work with Paul. Things were

good the first few years. We clicked. I was happy. We were happy.

Until things started to change. He became too wrapped up in work. Wanted to keep climbing the ladder to take over my dad's company.

Now, it's the biggest wedge between us. And now Kade is back and has stepped right into the mess that is my life.

As I start the van and head to the ranch, I try to push the thoughts of Kade out of my head. But how can I? He woke up emotions in me I haven't felt in years. And having to tell him about Poppy? I guess I didn't have to worry about telling him because he figured it out.

What's going to happen now? It's the thought that keeps plaguing me.

Poppy is the most important person in my life. I can't lose her. I don't know Kade anymore. What if he's angry and wants to take her from me?

I crack the windows, letting the fresh mountain air in to help soothe my frayed nerves.

I wonder what would have happened if Kade had stayed to fight for us. If he hadn't left town. Would we still be together? Would we be where we are now? At odds with one another?

Back when we first got together, I was so full of hope for our future. Every one of those dreams was dashed when he left.

Pulling under the gateway to the ranch, I follow the familiar road to the lodge. A few cars are in the guest parking lot, but it's not busy like it used to be.

God, it's been ages since I've been here.

I grab the large bags of food from the back of the truck and head inside.

"Hey, girl," Joey greets me. "Is that lunch? I'm starving and Rex is still working on his new menu."

Sam, the ranch hand, is standing behind her. I've seen him around town, but don't know him that well.

"You know it." I set the bags on top of the desk. "Is Kade around? I'm just going to let him know it was delivered."

"I'll take these to the dining room," Sam says, interrupting us with a wink to Joey.

"Is that all you want to do?" She waggles her brows at me.

"Stop it." I nudge her in the side before walking down the hall to the office. The door is cracked open, and Kade's warm voice filters out.

"I know I only said I'd be gone for a few weeks, but I need to extend my time off."

Time off?

I thought he was here for good.

"I don't know. Could be a while."

I'm only hearing his side of the conversation, so it's hard to know what he's discussing, but I think I get the gist.

"I'll still be taking calls and meetings. No balls have been dropped yet. I understand. Maybe February?"

Does that mean what I think it means? That Kade won't be here longer than a few months?

My stomach drops out at the thought of it. I don't realize the call has ended until Kade is bumping into me in the hall.

"Presley. What are you doing here?"

"Oh, um, hi," I stutter.

Kade is standing there in all his glory, in a tight plaid shirt with the sleeves rolled up. Jeans stretching across his thighs. And that same damn hat that would make even the most saintly woman swoon.

"Did Betty send you up here to bring lunch?"

I nod. Suddenly my mouth is too dry to even speak.

"Do you need help bringing it in?"

"No." I shake my head, clearing my throat. "It's taken care of."

"Good." He scrubs a hand over the back of his neck. "I appreciate you taking care of it."

"No problem." Passing through the lobby, I take in the space. "Looks like you've made some good changes in here."

"You think so?"

I nod. "I haven't been here in years, but it looks good."

A fresh coat of paint—the smell thick in the air—covers the walls. Photos of the ranch rest in shining frames. Even the wooden front desk has a new coat of varnish.

With the sun coming in through clean windows, it welcomes people to The Lost Spur.

"Thanks. It's going to take a lot more than this to get this place where it needs to be."

"Do you plan on sticking around to whip it into shape?"

"Why wouldn't I?" He flips his eyes back to me.

I come to an abrupt stop. "Relax. I don't know what your plans are. I only imagine you have a life back home."

"Right." He turns away from me, closing himself off to any emotions.

He heads to the dining room and I follow. I go to help Joey arrange all the dishes and utensils. It gives me something to do with my hands.

There was a time when Kade stirred the opposite reaction in me. Being around him now? I want to get everything sorted here then leave with my tail between my legs.

People from the ranch—people I recognize—start filtering inside to grab plates and get lunch. I smile at them, trying to keep my nerves at bay.

But when Kade appears behind me, I startle.

"Can I talk to you for a minute?" Kade asks.

I nod, wiping my hands off and following him to a small alcove by the kitchen. "Is everything okay?"

"Look, Pres." Kade rests his ass against a table, crossing his ankles as he faces me. "I want to know Poppy."

I suck in a deep breath. I knew this would be coming. I didn't know when, but I knew it would be. Because Kade is a good person, and why wouldn't he want to know his daughter?

With everything else going on in my life, what's one more complication?

"She doesn't know you're her dad," I say. "There's enough going on in her life right now."

"What's going on?" he questions.

I ignore the question—I don't need to get into my separation and issues with my dad's estate. "Enough that I don't want to add more stress to her plate. I get you want to know her, but I decide when she learns the truth."

His jaw ticks. He's not happy, but he nods his head. "I guess I'll take what I can get."

"Why don't I bring her by the ranch tomorrow? I have the day off with her."

"Okay."

"I mean it, Kade." His name feels foreign on my tongue. "That's the one nonnegotiable. You can't tell Poppy who you are. If you're not going to be sticking around—"

He stands, closing the distance between the two of us. "You keep saying that. I have responsibilities here now."

I steel my spine, tilting my chin up to face him. I won't back down from him. "You left once. Forgive me if I don't exactly trust you."

"And why did I leave, Presley?" He cocks his brow at me.

"It's not my fault." I poke a finger in his chest. "One minute you were here, the next you were gone."

Tension swirls between the two of us. It's that same feeling from the other night in the diner. Kade's eyes dart down to my mouth. I don't miss the way his tongue peeks out to wet his bottom lip.

How is it I can want someone who makes me so crazy? Except before either of us can close the distance between our mouths, a voice rounds the corner.

"Hey, boss?" comes a woman's voice.

I jump back, hitting my back against the corner of the wall.

"Yeah?" Kade scrubs a hand down his face, turning away from me.

"You're needed in the kitchen."

"Everything okay?"

"New appliances are here and you need to sign for them."

"Be right there, Reenie," he says, his voice raspy.

Reenie's gaze flits between the two of us. I rub the sore spot on my back as she leaves.

I clear my throat. "We'll be over after lunch if that works."

"Right."

I brush past him, ignoring the heat emanating from him. Before I can get far, he grabs my arm. Sparks shoot through me.

"Presley?"

"Yeah?"

Meeting his gaze, there is a softness there now.

"I...thanks. Thank you."

All I can do is nod and run out. Because anything else

will trigger all of my emotions about Kade. About that day I found out I was pregnant and wanted nothing more than to tell him about it.

Kade now knows about Poppy.

I only hope he treats her like the precious gift that she is. I couldn't take anything else.

Chapter Eleven

KADE

"You're looking awfully antsy there, boss," Sam says.

I check the stirrup one last time before adjusting the girth on Lollipop.

"Presley is bringing Poppy to the ranch today. I want her to have a good time." But then a worried thought hits me. "Can a kid her age even ride a horse?"

Lollipop chomps down on more hay, not a care in the world.

Sam laughs at me. "She'll be fine. I had Lennox on a horse at four. Poppy is going to love it."

"I hope so."

Because this is the first time I'm spending any kind of time with my daughter.

Daughter.

I still can't believe she's mine. That Presley and I have a kid together and I only just found out about it.

I try not to let that thought stoke my rage. I've already missed so much with her, and I don't want to lose any more time.

If getting to spend a few hours with Poppy means having to see Presley, so be it. It's not like anything is going to happen again.

That kiss?

I don't care how fucking good it was. How it awakened feelings in me that I haven't felt in years. Things I've only felt with Presley.

Sure, I've dated and had relationships while in Seattle. I wasn't going to become celibate just because I didn't have *her*.

But nothing ever felt as good as being with her.

I shut that thought down. Lock it up tight. I'm here for the ranch. And now Poppy. Everything else can be figured out later.

No more kisses or almost-kisses.

The sounds of footsteps grow closer. Spinning on my heel, I see Poppy running toward me with Presley following in her wake. At a much slower pace.

"Hi, Kade." She's out of breath by the time she stops in front of me.

Her blonde hair is in pigtails, and she's in a pink sweatshirt, jeans, and cowboy boots. She's fucking adorable.

"Hi, Poppy." I drop down to my knees to get on her level.

I have no idea how to interact with kids. I've never really been around them before. It's a whole new world for me.

"What are we going to do today?" she asks, bouncing on the balls of her feet.

"I thought maybe we could ride horses." My eyes dart to Presley's. "If it's okay with your mom."

Poppy runs over to her, jumping up and down. "Please, Mom? Can I ride the horse?"

"Only if you listen to Kade. You've never been on a horse, and I don't want you falling off."

"Yes!" She pumps her arm before coming back over to me. "She said yes."

"Follow me."

Poppy grabs my hand, walking beside me. It tugs on my heart as I lead her into the barn. It's not the worst start to this parenting thing.

"This is Lollipop."

Leading her up to the mare, we approach her from the front.

"Her name is Lollipop?" she asks, looking up at her in awe. "She doesn't look like a Lollipop."

"She's really sweet. I have a feeling she'll like you, but why don't we warm her up with a treat?"

"Okay."

Presley stays close, eyeing us as I grab a bag of carrots and pull one out. The horse's eyes track the movement, feet stamping on the ground.

"She's excited," Poppy tells me, still standing a few feet away from the horse.

"She likes treats. Hold your hand like this." I demonstrate how to hold it out flat. "I'll put the carrot on your palm and Lollipop will eat it, okay?"

She does as I tell her, and there's barely time to give her the carrot before Lollipop is sniffing at it before gobbling it down.

"Her mouth tickles." Poppy giggles as Lollipop chomps on the carrot.

"You're doing a really good job," I encourage.

"She's pretty."

"Do you want to pet her?"

"Yes." Poppy bobs her head up and down.

"You can rub her nose between her eyes."

Her face lights up with delight as Lollipop lets her pet her. So far, things seem to be going well. I mean, it could be worse. She could have run crying from the barn. Then any hope of a relationship with my daughter would go right out the window.

It probably helps that Poppy was talking to me before she even really met me.

"Let's grab you a helmet," I say.

Helping Poppy get the right size, I get her all buckled in before helping her on the horse. She looks fucking adorable sitting up there on Lollipop.

Grabbing the rope, I click at the horse and start leading the two of them around the ring. Presley is standing in the middle of the barn, a nervous look on her face.

Having done this before, I know how to do it. And with Lollipop being the sweetest horse on the ranch, Poppy is in good hands. Her hands are wrapped tight around the horn of the saddle.

"Are you liking it?" I ask Poppy.

"I really like it. Can we go faster?"

I shake my head. "Not today. If you want lessons, maybe your mom can bring you out to the ranch and I can teach you."

"I don't think Mom has ever ridden a horse before."

"She has," I answer without thinking.

"Really? Maybe she can ride with me."

I glance over to Presley. A memory crashes into my mind. One of when Presley and I took one of the older horses out for a ride. I had a picnic for the two of us. It was the first time we ever slept together. That was one of the best days of my life.

I miss those days. Now that I'm back in Pinecrest, it's harder to push aside the memories. Because everywhere I turn is steeped in history. The two of us were always joined at the hip. Where one of us went, the other was always there. There isn't a place that Presley and I haven't gone. Haven't shared something special together. I wish it didn't hurt, but it does.

Being here now makes me realize just how much I've missed out on.

"Hey Sam," I call out. "Want to help lead Poppy around the barn?"

"Sure thing, boss," he agrees.

"Sam's going to take you around the barn, okay? I'm going to talk to your mom."

"Make sure to tell her I want lessons," Poppy says.

I smile up at her. "I will."

Heading to where Presley is, I nod my head toward the benches on the side.

"Can I talk to you for a minute, Presley?"

"Sure."

She looks at me, eyes shifting, like she's nervous. That's new.

I drop down next to her. Our knees brush together and I ignore the swooping feeling in my gut. Nope, not going to think about that at all.

"What do you want to talk about?"

Presley pulls her knee back, tucking a lock of hair behind her ear.

Huh. Seems like she's not the only one feeling things.

"I'm not going to lie, Pres. I'm pissed. Really, really pissed." I turn to face her and she's looking down, picking at her fingernail. "I have a daughter that I didn't know about. It hurts."

"I tried, Kade. When I realized I was pregnant, I called you, but your number was disconnected. I went to your mom's and she didn't want to talk to me. Believe me, I tried. But you made it clear you didn't want anything to do with me, so I did what I had to."

"I've missed a lot and I don't want to miss anything else."

"Okay."

"And I—wait, okay?" I'm shocked. I thought she would put up more of a fight than this. "You're okay with it?"

Presley looks worried now.

"What's going on, Pres?"

"Look, if you're going to have a relationship with Pop, you and I have to be cordial." She ignores me.

I smirk at her. "I think we're being pretty cordial to one another right now."

"I mean…" She casts a glance to the ring to make sure Poppy is still riding. She is. "We can't have any more repeats of what happened at the diner."

"It was a mistake. It won't happen again," I agree.

Something flashes in her eyes. Did she expect me to fight her? It *was* a mistake. Sure, I have no idea what is going on in my life, but starting things with Presley? It'll only complicate matters.

"Good. I have a meeting Friday. Would you want to watch Poppy?"

"Yes." I jump at the chance. "I'd really like that."

Sam stops with Poppy in front of us and helps her down. She comes running over, head bobbing under her helmet, and throws her arms around Presley.

"Did you see me, Mom? That was so much fun."

"You did great, baby." She unclicks the helmet and presses a kiss to her cheek. "What do you say to Kade?"

"Thank you." She turns her attention to me and throws her arms around me. "That was the mostest fun ever!"

"I'm glad you had fun." Fuck. That makes my heart grow two sizes. "I have something for you, Poppy."

"You do?" she asks, looking up at me.

"I do."

Jogging back into the office, I grab the hat off its hook and head back into the ring. Poppy is standing next to Presley. The two of them are playing some game with their hands. Watching them together, it's easy to see how much they love each other.

I'm glad Presley is going to let me have a relationship with her. Because I don't want to lose any more time with Poppy. I want what they have. It might take a while to get there, but I'm here. I'm not going anywhere. Well, at least for the time being.

"This is for you."

I hold the hat in my hands out for Poppy, and her eyes light up with happiness. "Really?"

It's a small, beige cowgirl hat. She wastes no time plopping it right on her head.

"You look like a cowgirl," I say.

"This is so cool. Thanks."

Poppy wraps her arms around me and damn, I really could get used to this.

"What do you say about coming back here on Friday, Poppy, and hanging out with Kade?"

She nods her head with a ferocity, the hat falling off. "That would be so much fun."

"Good." I smile down at her. "I'll make sure Lollipop is ready to go."

"Yes."

She waves to me before going to say goodbye to Lollipop, leaving Presley and me in an awkward silence.

"Thanks for bringing her out here," I say, stuffing my hands in my jean pockets.

"Sure. We'll see you Friday."

Presley spins, grabbing Poppy by the hand and leading her out of the barn.

Well, things could have been worse. Poppy could have hated me right out of the gate and never wanted to come back.

I guess things with both of them might go better than I thought.

Chapter Twelve

KADE

"Joey, can I ask you something?"

Walking up to the front desk, I drop off the box of paint samples on the counter and lean over. I get an irritated look from her. Considering I'm her boss, it's pretty bold of her. Considering she's Presley's best friend?

I still expect it. I'll deal with it. Eventually I'll win her over.

"What is it?" Her tone is more polite.

"What would a five-year-old like to do?"

"Huh?" She looks confused.

"Poppy is coming by this afternoon, and I don't know what to do with her," I confess.

"Didn't you take her riding the other day?" she asks. "Kids love horses."

"I already did that. I want to do something different with her."

"Hiking? Archery? Fishing?"

"Fishing?" That piques my interest. "Would she like fishing?"

This time, I get a smile from Joey. "I think she'll like it.

Poppy isn't your average girl. She likes doing everything. And I mean *everything*."

Fishing. I wouldn't have thought of it, but I always liked fishing. It was something I was good at. Verne would take me out in his boat and we'd float for hours. Sometimes, we didn't catch anything, but we'd enjoy each other's company. Those days with him were some of my favorite.

Maybe Poppy will enjoy it like I did.

I rap my knuckles against the counter. "Thanks, Joey."

As I start to walk away, she calls me back before I can leave.

"Kade."

I stop, spinning on my heel to face her again. "Yeah?"

"Don't hurt them. They've been through a lot and they deserve to be happy. Both of them."

Why the fuck is everyone being so cryptic? I keep hearing about what they're going through, but what the fuck? Have I really missed that much in the years I've been gone?

I scrub a hand down my face. It's fucking driving me crazy that I don't know what's going on in their lives.

Am I even entitled to it?

Heading out front, I bypass the workers bringing in supplies to work on the guest rooms and wait for Poppy. Her babysitter is dropping her off today.

I'm excited that she's coming. That Presley is trusting me with her. A blue car pulls up around the driveway, Poppy's excited face peering at me from the backseat. Complete with her cowgirl hat.

I wave at the nanny before Poppy bursts out of the car.

"Hi, Kade."

"Hey, Poppy." I kneel down, holding my hand out for a high five, which she happily returns. "Ready for more fun things at the ranch?"

"Why's it called The Lost Spur?"

I look at her babysitter. "She asked when we came in. I said you would know. I'm Becca, by the way."

"Kade." I stick my hand out for her to shake.

"Nice to meet you. Have fun with Kade, Poppy. I'll see you tomorrow."

"Bye, Becca!" Poppy calls back to her before turning to face me.

I tap a finger on my chin. "So, why is it called The Lost Spur?"

"Do you know?" She adjusts her hat.

"You know those metal things on cowboy boots?"

She nods. "Mr. Verne used to wear them."

"He lost one of his one time, so he walked around town with only one on his boots. He looked funny, and people laughed at him. He thought it'd be funny to name his ranch that."

Poppy giggles. It's the sweetest damn sound, and I love that she's at ease with me. "Did he ever find it?"

"You know, I don't know," I answer honestly. "Are you ready for the activity we'll be doing today?"

"Are we going to see Lollipop? I drew her picture at school." Setting her backpack down, she fishes out a piece of paper and hands it over to me. There's a brown blob in the middle with two stick figures on either side. "That's us with her."

"Wow, this looks great."

She smiles. "I made it for you."

I swallow back the emotion that threatens to take over. "Thanks, Poppy. I'll have to show Lollipop later, but today I thought we could go fishing."

"Fishing?" She screws her nose up as she slings her backpack over her shoulder. "I've never been fishing. Aren't they slimy?"

Grabbing her hand, I lead her down to the lake that sits near the front of the property. It's a short walk and doesn't take us long, even adjusting my stride to her smaller steps.

"We'll catch them then throw them back."

"We're not going to eat them? I like fish sticks."

I hold back my laughter. "These aren't the kind of fish you eat in those. But I have a feeling you'll have fun."

Poppy shrugs a shoulder as the old shack that holds the fishing gear comes into view. "Okay."

I find a small pair of waders and boots for Poppy to wear and grab the fishing lines to head out to the canoe.

"Now, I want you to stay seated, okay? Can you swim?" I ask as I buckle her life jacket.

She nods. "Mom takes me when it's hot outside to the pool."

"I'll thread your line and show you how to cast it."

"What's casting mean?" she asks.

"It's how you throw your bait in to try and catch a fish." I mimic the move. "The farther away, the easier it is to draw them in. We want to be nice and quiet so we don't scare them off."

"I can be quiet," she whispers, to prove her point.

"Good job." I give her a high five. "Let's get out there."

Poppy chatters away about her day, telling me about her friends as we get farther away from the shore. I don't know who any of the people she's talking about are, but I love hearing about her day.

Finding a good spot, I come to a stop and grab the tackle box and our poles.

"Pick a lure and I'll help you bait your line and then we'll cast them."

Poppy picks a bright orange one and I show her how to

do everything. She's a natural as her line sails into the water.

"Did I do it right?"

"You did. Great job."

"Did you do this with your dad?" she asks.

Poppy is full of questions.

I shake my head. "My dad wasn't around much when I was your age. But you know who showed me how to fish?"

"Who?"

"Verne."

She giggles. "Mr. Verne liked Miss Betty's secret milkshake."

"What's a secret milkshake?"

"It's a secret." I don't miss the duh in her tone.

"Right."

"My dad hasn't taken me fishing."

If only she knew.

"Do you want him to take you fishing?"

She shakes her head. "No. Because he makes Mom sad."

"He does?" I ask, turning my attention to my daughter. She's sitting cross-legged in the boat.

She nods. "Ever since we left Dad. He made her sad, so we left."

Dad. It hurts to hear her call someone else that when I'm her *actual* father. When that douche Paul got this time with her. He doesn't deserve her. Hell, he doesn't deserve either one of them.

"She left?"

"Mom said we were getting a new house, but Dad wasn't coming. It was after Grandpa died."

"Your grandpa died?"

That's news to me.

"Yeah, but he wasn't fun. I couldn't do anything at his house because I'd get in trouble if I broke something."

"I'm sorry, Poppy."

I don't know how long Presley and Poppy have been on their own, but I hate that Poppy had to worry about these kinds of things. Chalk it up to another reason I hated Presley's dad. If he were here now, he wouldn't approve of me spending time with Poppy or Presley.

He'd do everything in his power to get me to stay away from them.

The bastard.

"Being here is fun," she says, a smile brightening her face before her rod tugs. "Did I catch one?"

"Yes." Dropping my pole to the side, I cover her hands with mine and slowly start to reel him in. The closer he gets to the boat, the more he thrashes.

"I can see him!" Poppy points to him. "He's huge."

"You did good, Pop."

By the time I find the basket to catch him, Poppy is squealing. Pulling him out, he's at least eight inches long.

"He's huge!"

"Can you believe you caught him?"

"I'm the best fisher girl in the world."

"Damn right you are. You want to hold him?"

Her blue eyes go wide. "Will he be slimy?"

"Scaly and wet, but it'll be okay."

She holds her hands out and I pass him over.

"It's weird," she says.

"We need to throw him back in a minute."

"Can I name him first?" she asks.

"Sure. Let me snap a picture of you holding him for your mom."

"Frankie. His name is Frankie," she tells me.

She holds out the fish, her smile taking up her entire

face as I take the photo. It's the cutest thing ever. Poppy is beaming with pride as I help her put him back in the water.

"I can't wait to tell Mom!"

She helps me with baiting and recasting her line, and a happy smile settles on my face.

Fishing with my daughter.

I never thought that this would be my life. By the time I moved to Seattle, I put kids and any kind of future where I was happy out of my mind. If I didn't have Presley, I didn't see the point of having a family.

But this? This feels pretty damn good. And is reminiscent of days with Verne.

One of the reasons I loved fishing with Verne was getting to talk to him. Some days, we didn't speak more than two words to one another. Other days, if I was having issues with Presley's parents, I'd vent to him. He was there for me more than my dad ever was. Getting some version of what's going on with Presley from Poppy, even from her point of view, makes me want to know more. Makes me want to be here for my daughter.

Whatever Poppy needs, I'll be there for her. No questions asked.

Except to get to the bottom of what's going on with Presley.

That requires a lot of questions. Ones I hope I can get answers to today.

Chapter Thirteen

PRESLEY

Another meeting. Another meeting where nothing will get resolved but they'll say they're working on settling Dad's estate.

I hate these days. Having to step into a pencil skirt and a stiff blouse, it takes everything I have to put on a mask to deal with Paul and my mother.

Flipping down the visor in my old beat-up truck, I check my makeup one last time. At least if I look good, that will be one less thing for my mother to nitpick.

It's about as good as it's going to get. After working at the diner this morning, I left early to come home and change before driving to the way too modern office for Pinecrest. Of course Dad would use them. The higher the price tag, the more interested he was.

Grabbing my purse, I push open the creaking door and head inside. Paul and my mother are waiting in the marble lobby.

It's so stuffy. I get quick, disapproving glances from both of them, without any other conversation.

Just as well. I take a seat opposite them and wait.

And wait. And *wait*.

What the hell is the point of scheduling a meeting if you're going to be late? I don't want to be here a minute longer than I have to be.

"Mrs. King. Mr. Leith. Ms. King. We're ready for you."

A young woman with a slicked back bun and a black pantsuit clacks her way into the lobby to beckon us back to a conference room.

It's even more gaudy than the lobby. Dark hardwood lines every surface in the room with awards hanging from the walls.

It's pretentious.

"Good afternoon, everyone," Mr. Tartt greets us.

An older gentleman with wire-rimmed glasses and a thin mustache, he is not someone to mess with. His ego fills the entire room.

Someone my dad liked.

"I want to thank you all for coming today to discuss the estate of Mr. King. We do have some updates for you."

"Are we any closer to closing this out?" I ask, not wanting to beat around the bush.

"Presley," Paul snaps. "Show the man the respect he is due."

Crossing my arms, I lean back in my chair, shaking my head. Why does Paul make me feel like such a teenager needing to be scolded?

We keep having these unnecessary meetings. Close, but not there yet. Still waiting on the value of whatever property my dad had.

Why do I have to take the day off work to come out here and deal with this?

"It's okay, Mr. Leith. We are close, but not quite there."

I sigh. Of course. I shouldn't be surprised. At the rate

this is going, it's going to take the full two years in probate before everything gets resolved.

"Was the accountant I sent your way helpful?" Paul asks, leaning over the table.

Staring at my ex brings up too many emotions. This is the only time I've spent with him in the last year—in lawyers' offices.

"As I explained to your assistant, Mr. Leith, we have our own in-house accountants. They are working with King Properties to ensure the value of all assets is recorded correctly."

"Do you know how much longer this is going to take?" Mom asks.

"Mrs. King, it's unknown how long this will take. Your husband's company has a high value with several arms that need to be reviewed. We do not want to make any judgments based on information provided at the time of his will review two years ago."

Paul scoffs. "Unbelievable."

"What's wrong, Paul?" I ask.

I shouldn't egg him on, but I do.

He turns his ire to me. With slicked back brown hair and dark eyes, I don't know why I ever found him attractive. Not when his personality is the same as a slimy snake.

"The company should be mine," he hisses, stabbing a finger on the table. "Your father wanted me to have it."

"But he didn't," I state calmly. "He left it to me."

"Why do you want it so badly?" he asks. "You don't want it. You hated your dad."

"So that makes it okay for you to take everything from me?"

"You're the one that's taking everything from me, Presley. Grow up and be an adult about this."

Fire blazes through me. "I *am* being an adult, Paul. I'm doing what's best for me and my daughter."

"Ms. King." The attorney looks to me. "As we've discussed, you can sign over King Properties to Mr. Leith."

"So he can take everything I have?"

"I want what I want, Presley. You know my terms," he says again.

I hate this man. I don't know how I ever tried to make things work with him. He wants the company and to leave me with nothing. But if I don't give it to him? He's going to try and get joint custody of Poppy, wanting to poison her against me.

I'm between a rock and a hard place. Because until everything gets cleared with my father's estate, I'm in limbo. I'm working at the diner to make ends meet because even with the distributions from the company, it's hard. And my soon-to-be ex isn't doing anything to help.

"And I'm not doing anything until the estate is settled."

"Presley, enough of this," Mom snaps. "Stop acting like a child and go home to your husband. Let Paul run the company and take care of you."

"Take care of me? You mean stay in a loveless marriage?"

Mom waves me off. "You want to be taken care of. Paul will do that."

"I'm doing just fine taking care of myself and Poppy."

"At a diner? Please, Presley." Mom narrows her gaze at me. "That is not suitable for a King."

"It works for me." I turn my attention to the lawyer before standing. "Mr. Tartt. Please don't call me unless the estate is settled. If you need to pass along updates, email me."

I give one last look to my mom and Paul before storming out.

I can't handle the person the two of them turn me into.

Tossing my bag into the front seat of my truck, I turn the car toward the diner. At least there's a light at the end of this miserable afternoon.

Poppy. And if I'm telling the truth, a part of me—a small part of me—wants to see Kade again.

My life is a disaster. I need to get everything in order before I even let myself think these thoughts. But I can't help it.

Because Kade is back in town.

And what happens next? Maybe we'll be able to get back a part of ourselves that we lost that fateful night.

Chapter Fourteen

PRESLEY - SIX YEARS EARLIER

PRESLEY

I can't wait to see you tonight

KADE

Not as much as I want to see you

If only you were my date, Bubs

One of these days, I'll be hubs

Until there's a ring on it, Bubs, you're the boyfriend, not the hubs

Just you wait, Pres

You won't know what'll hit you

Well, I'll just be waiting around for you until I get my ring

As long as you're waiting for me at the end of the night

You know I will be

> I wish you weren't working the event

> Have to make that money if I'm going to get you the ring you deserve

> I don't need a fancy ring

> Just you

> I love you

> I love you too

> See you soon 😭

I smooth my hands down the front of my green dress. There's some big announcement for King Properties tonight. What it's for? I don't know.

But my presence is required. One of the many duties as my parents' daughter.

I sigh, looking around the opulent ballroom. I detest everything my parents stand for. I don't like these parties. I hate the way they flaunt their money, holding it over others in town to bend to their will.

I sip on an iced tea in the corner, making small talk with those that come over to me. These people think I'll put in a good word with my parents, but they don't know that I have no input in the business.

It's a Saturday night. It's my senior year and I'd rather be anywhere but here. All of my friends went out to the lake on the ranch. Did I get to go?

No.

At least I'm not alone. My eyes find Kade's as he serves the guests. One of the jobs he has when he's home from college. None of them notice him, but I do. I always notice him.

"Ma'am. Would you like a…thing?" Kade smiles at me as he walks up to me.

"That's not what I want."

"Anything I can do to quench your need right *now*?"

There's a tease in his voice. "At the moment? I don't think it'd be appropriate."

"Presley…"

"Excuse me. Can I get another drink?" A woman interrupts us, tapping Kade on the shoulder.

"Yes, ma'am. What would you like?"

"A chardonnay, please."

"One moment."

Kade leaves to go fill her order while she chats my ear off about the latest property that my dad is looking to purchase.

I give her a polite smile, nodding along like I'm interested. Maybe if my parents had another kid, hell if they had a boy, I might not have to be here right now.

"Make sure to tell your father."

I smile. "I will."

"Good to see you, Presley."

Before I can sneak away to try and find Kade again, Mom is at my side.

"Presley, dear. We need you." Mom grasps my elbow and pulls me toward the makeshift stage.

I set my drink on a table and trail behind her.

Only a few more hours and then I can cut out of here and meet the girls. There's a bonfire going on where they are at the moment. If I had my phone with me, I'm sure I'd be getting all the pictures. Especially since Joey's latest crush is there.

"Where have you been?" Dad scolds by the time I flank him on the stage.

"Mingling with your guests."

My smile is stiff, but polite. Now that we're on stage, all eyes are on us.

"Let's get started," Mom says, trying to push us away from a confrontation.

Dad pulls notecards from his pocket as one of his faithful employees joins us on stage.

I wonder what he's doing here. Probably going to be announced the lead of some new project.

When the stage lights turn up, I paste a fake smile on.

"Thank you all for joining us here this evening," Dad greets.

He drones on about the great year the company is having. It's everything I've heard at dinner these last few weeks. No matter what I want to do, I have to be at the dinner table every day at seven.

"Not only is it a great night for King Properties, but for the King family as well."

That piques my interest. What in the world is going on? My eyes track Kade, still serving everyone with a smile.

Just like him.

"I am pleased to announce the engagement of our daughter to Paul Leith."

"What?" Dread fills my stomach as my gaze snaps to my father's.

"Get over there," Mom hisses out of the corner of her mouth. "Don't be rude."

"What is going on?" I ask, not budging. "Engagement?"

"We've been looking forward to Paul joining our family as our future son-in-law."

Glasses shatter in the back of the ballroom. Kade's eyes are on mine, fire blazing.

"Kade."

I try to go to him, but a hand stops me. I don't know how long the two of us stay locked like this. Pain is etching itself into my cells at the sheer heartbreak on his face. My lip quivers as the room blurs. I blink and Kade is gone.

"Presley. You have to stay here. This is no way to handle your engagement."

I rip my arm from hers. "That would imply I knew I was getting engaged tonight."

Lifting the hem of my dress, I bolt from the ballroom. It's not busy at the valet stand, with only a few people lingering.

"Kade!" I call out. "Kade!"

No matter which way I turn, he isn't there. How could he have gotten out of here so fast?

Tears are streaking down my face. I kick off my heels and run down the sidewalk. There is no sign of him.

"Kade!"

What the hell is going on? Kade is gone and I'm *engaged* to Paul? When the night started, my biggest concern was getting out of here as fast as I could so Kade and I could go to the bonfire.

In one short speech, everything has changed.

"Kade."

It's a plea. A cry to will him to find me. My heart is breaking. Where is the man I love?

"Presley Ann King." Mom's voice is furious. "You need to get inside right now and stop embarrassing me and your father."

"What did you do?"

"What we needed to."

"Needed to?" I wipe an angry tear from my face. "Why?"

"You were going to throw your life away on that man. We couldn't let you do that."

It's like a slap to the face. "I wasn't throwing my life away."

"Not anymore." Mom grabs my wrist. "Get inside now, clean yourself up, and act like a happy woman who is engaged."

I'm going to be sick.

Engaged?

Nausea boils in my belly. My entire body is numb as I'm dragged back inside. *Where did he go?*

I don't know what's happening, but I'm going to figure this out and find Kade. It's all I can think about. It's not a happy thought, but it'll get me through the rest of this night.

Because all that matters is Kade.

Nothing else.

Chapter Fifteen

KADE

"Are you sure you don't want any help?" Reenie asks.

I shake my head, standing in the doorway to my office. My still very messy office.

"I wouldn't know what to keep or not unless I look at it. If you don't see me in a few hours, send help."

She smiles at me. "I'll bring you lunch then and make sure the filing cabinet didn't topple over on you."

"Appreciate it."

She closes the door behind her and I let out a breath. Fuck. I have no idea where I'm even going to start.

The filing cabinet in the corner is likely my best bet. With papers sticking out in every direction, I start with one drawer at a time.

Pulling it open, I gather everything inside and start flipping through it.

Invoices from at least ten years ago. Old guest reservations. A few menus with the pages curling up from age. Hell, there's even old plans to renovate his house. I tuck those away. Maybe it's something I can look into later.

Ranch first. It's been my motto since I got here. Even if it's slipping because of Presley and Poppy.

I can't think about them right now. Right now, I need to tackle this space so I can get some actual work done. Grabbing the garbage bin, I start throwing things in. No time to be sentimental. If I have any hope of finding things in here that are useful, I need to be savage and trash everything.

But a few things here and there I keep. Like what appears to be one of the first room keys to room one.

"You sentimental old bastard." I smile at the heavy key in my hand.

I tuck it into my front pocket so it doesn't get lost in the mess.

The morning goes by in a blur of stacks of shit to throw out and more paper cuts than I care to admit to.

By the time my stomach starts to growl, I've finally found something useful. Some recent profit and loss statements that can help me see what Verne was doing.

A knock sounds from the door and I drop the papers in my hands.

Thank God. I'm starving.

"Got a minute?"

My gaze snaps to the door. Not Reenie bringing me my lunch, but…

"Presley. Hi." I wave her in. "Find a seat if you can."

She lifts a stack of papers off the rickety folding chair. "Doing some spring cleaning?"

I laugh. "More like a complete gut job. I don't know the last time Verne went through everything in here."

"Looks like you have your work cut out for you."

I smile at her. It feels easy to do now that there's this mutual understanding between the two of us.

"Did you need something?"

She wipes her hands on her jeans. Her coat is zipped up, but I can see the hint of her pink collared shirt underneath. Her long blonde hair is still tied up in her bandanna.

"I wanted to talk to you about Poppy."

"Is everything okay?"

"Yeah. But I was wondering if you'd want to start taking her after school a few days a week."

"Really?"

She nods. "Yes. You want to get to know her, and with my babysitter's schedule changing, it'd help me too."

"You trust me with her?"

"You're her father."

It isn't a rave review of trust, but at least it's something.

"I can make things work."

"Are you sure?" she questions. "I don't want you to get busy and then leave her with someone else here. It would kind of defeat the purpose of you getting to know her."

"I'll make time for her, Presley."

If I have to move meetings around in the afternoon, so be it. I might not always have the most flexible of schedules if I have a difficult client, but I'll make it happen. Because like Presley said, I want a relationship with my daughter. I'm not passing her off to anyone here to help.

"She likes you, so I don't think it'll be too hard for you."

I smile at the woman across from me. It seems the icy walls around her heart are slowly melting.

"And if I start to lose her, there's always Lollipop."

"See? You'll do fine." She waves a hand around in the air. "And if you leave—"

"Right now, I'm staying."

"You are?"

I nod. "At least for a while."

I lean back in my chair, studying the woman in front of me. I have no doubt that it took a lot for her to come here and have this conversation with me. And while I still have no idea what my future holds in Pinecrest, I'll be there for my daughter.

"Will starting tomorrow work? Her babysitter can drop her off after school."

"Sounds great."

"Do you need any help in here?" she asks, standing and looking around the office as if seeing it for the first time.

"Why would you want to help me out in here?"

Presley smirks. "You were never one to keep things organized, Kade."

"Hey." I point a finger at her. "This is all Verne's doing."

"Sure. Blame the man that can't stand up for himself."

I walk over to the filing cabinet. "I mean, look at this. Who keeps a menu from twenty years ago?"

"Verne was sentimental."

Presley takes it from my hands and looks it over. "You know, it could be a cool thing to bring back to the ranch."

"What, food?" I snort laugh.

"No." She smacks my chest. The lightest brush of her hand against mine makes my heart clatter in my chest. "Do an old-school night. Bring back some traditions from the ranch of the early days."

I roll the idea around in my head. "Huh. That's not terrible."

"Gee, thanks, Kade."

She shuffles through some more papers in the bottom drawer, dropping to the floor and crossing her legs under her.

"We'd have to get some more paying guests to do that first."

"They'll come."

"You sound pretty confident there."

She's not looking at me, but going through what's now in her lap.

"Look at these," Presley says.

"What are they?"

Dropping to my knees, I peek over her shoulder, doing my best not to get too close. To not breathe her in or feel her warmth.

"Old pictures of the ranch."

Plucking one out of her fingers that she passes over, I'm struck with warmth and sadness all at once. Because, in a grainy old photo, Verne and Arlene are standing under the ranch gateway with their arms wrapped around one another. Arlene is looking at the camera, hand covering her eyes from the sun while Verne stares down at her with his cigarette hanging out of his mouth.

"I can't imagine how old this is."

"Seventy-nine, it looks like." Presley pokes her finger at the back of the photo. "Wasn't that around when the ranch opened?"

"A few years after," I say.

"You should frame these. There's dozens of them, and people would love to see the ranch in the early days," Presley says, pulling the picture back into her hand.

Her fingertips brush mine, and I don't miss the tiny gasp it elicits from her.

Fuck.

I also don't miss the way it makes me feel. The rush of heat that floods my body. The memory of how her touch made me feel. The way I only thought about this woman for *years*.

"I should probably go."

It's barely more than a whisper. All I want to do is lean in and kiss her again. I want to feel her against me.

But that's not why she came.

"Right." I clear my throat, standing to put some air between us. "I need to grab some lunch before I get back to it."

Presley hands over the stack of photos, and I reach out a hand to help her up. She hesitates before taking it. That same buzzy feeling floats through me.

"I'll have Becca drop Poppy off tomorrow and then I can come grab her after my shift."

"I need to head into town, so I'll drop her off at the diner."

"I appreciate it, Kade."

"Hey." I grab her elbow, not letting her leave quite yet. "Thank *you*. I know this whole situation is weird, but… thank you for letting me have this time getting to know Poppy."

It looks like she wants to say something, her mouth opening and closing, but then she shuts it and leaves.

Damn. I don't know what she wanted to say, but I wish I could have made her stay. It's the first time I've wanted that since being back home.

As much as I want to focus on Presley, between my job in Seattle, the ranch, and now Poppy, I don't know where I'd find the time.

But I'm in Pinecrest. I'm here. Sure, the ranch brought me back to town, but Poppy and Presley? The only way I can work things out with them is by staying here.

It pulls a smile to my face. I guess it's something I don't mind as much as I thought I did. Getting to see Presley *more*?

I'll take whatever I can get.

Chapter Sixteen

PRESLEY

Tapping the screen on my phone, I check the time again. Ten minutes late. Kade was supposed to be here right at five, but they're late.

When it comes to Poppy, I'm not the most patient of people. It takes a lot for me to trust her with other people, and there aren't many who qualify. I want Kade to be one of them since he's her father, but it's hard.

God, is it ever hard to trust your kid with others.

Before I can send out a search party, the chime above the door tinkles and she bursts inside, Kade strutting behind her.

"Mom!" Poppy spots me, dashing into the diner. "We had so much fun today. Kade took me hiking."

"What?" I gasp. "That sounds like so much fun."

She pushes the wisps of hair out of her face. "He showed me the state tree and they smell like vanilla!"

"Wow. That is so cool."

"They were so big."

"Are you excited that you get to spend time at the ranch?"

She nods. "I love it. Kade is super fun."

The man in question smiles behind her.

"I'm glad you had fun. Why don't you go tell Betty about your day so I can talk to Kade?"

"Okay."

"Make sure to check that no one is coming out of the kitchen."

She darts off, leaving Kade and me alone.

"How did things go?" I ask as I motion him over to sit in an empty booth.

"Good. Sorry we're late. Poppy wanted to feed Lollipop before we left."

I smile at him. "I'm glad you had a good day with her."

"It was a good day." Kade leans back in the booth, draping an arm across the leather seat. "Poppy mentioned some things when we were fishing, but brought them up again today."

"Some things?"

He nods. "That you've been sad ever since you left Paul and your dad died."

I wince. "That's a very abbreviated version."

"Presley." Kade's voice is stern. "What happened?"

I'm nervous. I shouldn't be nervous around Kade, but I am. Because I don't want him to hate me anymore. Because we've had a few conversations together without it feeling like the world is going to end. I don't want what I tell him now to change things.

"My dad died about six months ago."

Kade reaches around, clasping a warm hand over mine. "I'm sorry, Pres. I can't imagine how hard that was."

I give him a sad smile. "I tried to have a relationship with him, but no matter what I did, it wasn't good enough for him. I wasn't a good enough wife to Paul. I was failing

Poppy because I wasn't putting her in all the extracurricular activities to improve her skills. I was letting her have playdates with other kids from families he didn't approve of." I scoff, tears welling in my eyes. "I hated it. I didn't want her to have the same childhood as me. But when he got sicker, and Paul started taking over, everything changed."

"What changed?" he asks, prodding me along.

"Paul wasn't around. He spent more time at work than at home. It was only me and Poppy. My mom would come around, but it would be to judge how dirty the house was or how I wasn't feeding her right."

"Jesus."

I remember how they treated Kade when we were dating. They looked down their noses at him. Like he was the scum on their shoe. I hated it. Kade dealt with it for me, but eventually, he stopped coming around.

I snuck out to see him, but my dad? He'd had enough. So he arranged for me to marry Paul.

Causing Kade to flee.

It was the last time I had anything resembling a relationship with my dad.

"I tried to be the person they wanted me to be, but nothing worked. Everything fell apart. I never had a great relationship with any of them. I didn't want to be a person that hated my life, so I took Poppy and left. Paul and I are legally separated, but then my dad died."

"What happened with his company?" Kade asks.

"That's the sticky situation. He never updated his will, so it still comes to me."

"Still?"

I nod. "Everything is still up in the air because his lawyers are still working out all the details of his estate. Because the company is in my name, I'm getting payouts from it. It's why I can afford to live and work right now. Paul hates it. He is trying to sue me for sole control."

"And if you don't give it to him?"

I wince. "He'll fight for joint custody of Poppy."

"So give it to him."

"I can't. I'll have nothing. Living on my own and trying to raise Poppy? It's not easy, and working at the diner wouldn't make ends meet."

Kade shakes his head, squeezing my hand. "I'm sorry, Presley. I really am."

I pull my hands back, not wanting his pity, and rest them in my lap. "And that's my sad story."

"Go out with me."

"What?" My gaze snaps to Kade's.

There's no pity there. What emotion is there, I can't quite pinpoint, but it's something that has my insides swirling.

"You heard me, Pres. Go out with me."

"You really want to go out with me?"

Every single reason I shouldn't go out with him flashes through my mind.

I'm not divorced yet.

My life is in flux.

I have Poppy to think about.

But no never crosses my lips.

"Yes. But Kade?"

"Yeah?"

"You're really good at leaving, Kade. Think you could try staying?"

Leaning across the table, he gives me the smile that won me over at fourteen. "For you? Yeah, I can try, Pres."

Pres.

I love how my name rolls off his tongue. Sweet, like

he's savoring it. Like he didn't get to say it for so long, so he wants to enjoy it while he can.

"You really want to go out with me?" I ask again.

"Are you trying to talk me out of this, Pres?" He grins at me.

I shake my head. "No. I just...haven't been on a first date in a long time."

"I promise, I'll make it worth your while."

I want to swoon. This is the Kade that I fell in love with. The one that could look at me and make me feel loved, safe, and happy with a single glance.

I couldn't resist him then and I don't want to resist him now. Not after everything we've been through. I want to capture that feeling of joy again.

"Well, with that kind of promise, who can say no?"

Chapter Seventeen

PRESLEY

No. No. Ugh, definitely no.

Why don't I own anything that would work for a first date?

Not just any first date. A first date with *Kade*.

The sound of laughter filters into my room. Poppy is watching cartoons in the living room before the babysitter comes over tonight.

Well, Betty. Because my normal girl is gone for the night.

Fishing my phone out from the pile of clothes littering my bed, I fire off a text.

> **PRESLEY**
> Help!
>
> What should I wear tonight?
>
> **GEORGIA**
> Need us to come over and help?
>
> Please

> **JOEY**
> Already on our way
>
> **JOEY**
> I have Max with me
>
> **RYLEE**
> Good
>
> **RYLEE**
> Aunt Rylee needs some snuggles
>
> **GEORGIA**
> But also help Pres for her first date
>
> **RYLEE**
> That too

> You guys are life savers

TOSSING my phone to the side, I tighten my robe around me and head into the kitchen. "You ready for some dinner, Pop?"

"What am I having?"

"How about your egg scramble you like?"

She nods, flipping back around on the couch. "Okay."

Making her dinner helps distract me from the matter at hand. I blow out a breath as I pour the eggs into a hot pan with peppers and spinach. For being a picky eater, Poppy likes weird things. Thank God she didn't fight me on what she wanted, since I'm a bit stressed out about my evening plans. Going on a first date with my high school sweetheart.

With *Kade*.

This could either be a great thing or a terrible idea.

When we talked at the diner the other day, the last

words I ever expected came out of his mouth. A date? I'm trying to keep the nerves at bay because I want it to go well.

What if we start to rehash the past and things go badly? It wouldn't just be me now that it affects. It'd be Poppy too.

Am I being selfish going out with him? Maybe we should just keep things friendly for our daughter. Before I can second-guess myself anymore, a knock sounds at the door as I'm scooping the scramble onto a plate.

"Hi, Aunt Joey. Hi, Max," Poppy greets them.

Max and Poppy head to the couch to watch a show they both like, playing with the stuffy that Max brought.

"I could hear you overthinking this from miles away," Joey says, laughing.

"Ugh. I can't help it. Does Max want anything to eat?"

Joey shakes her head. "I'm taking him to dinner with my parents after."

"Okay."

Walking over to the sofa, I hand Poppy her plate and press a kiss to her head before heading back to my room with Joey.

"Alright. What are your options?" Joey plops down on the clothes-covered bed.

"I have no idea." I blow out a frustrated breath. "Nothing I have is appropriate for a first date."

"What are the two of you doing?" Joey asks as the front door opens again and Rylee's excited squeal precedes her. Georgia's voice also floats through the air.

"Hi, babes." Georgia bobs into the room with clothes in her arms. "I figured I should bring some things for you because you'd hate everything you have."

I drop a peck on her cheek. "How'd you know?"

"Please. I sensed your nerves over the phone."

I smack a hand to my face. "Am I really that obvious?"

"Yes," they all answer in in unison.

"Can you blame me? I've been with two men my entire life. One of them being Kade. What if things have changed?"

"They have," Rylee points out.

"Thanks for the vote of confidence." I roll my eyes at her.

"It has though. You have a daughter. Kade is back in town. It's naïve to think things haven't changed. But how do you feel about him, Pres?" Georgia asks.

How do I feel about Kade?

Like he's been the missing piece all these years. That no matter how much I tried to move on from him, he was always there, floating in the background. My life was mostly good, but there was always something that wasn't complete.

"Clearly feelings are still there," Rylee says.

"How do you know?"

"That look on your face? It's easy to see how you still feel about him."

"I agree," Joey says. "Don't force things and take it easy. I promise, it'll be okay. Canceling at this point will do more harm than good."

I smile at them, sitting on the bed. "How'd you know I was considering it?"

"I could see it written all over your face."

"I don't want things between the two of us to affect Pop. He wants to have a relationship with her."

"And he will." Rylee squeezes my hand. "Now, stop stalling and try on some of these clothes."

"Try the green sweater first," Georgia says. "I think the off the shoulder will drive Kade nuts."

"Okay."

Heading into the bathroom, I slip off my robe and pull the sweater on over my head, giving my hair a fluff.

Paired with my jeans and a light coat of makeup, it looks amazing.

"Stop stalling and come out!" Joey calls. "We want to see how you look."

Stepping out of the bathroom, I'm met with cheers and catcalls.

"Damn, girl."

"Kade is going to lose his mind."

"You look *hot*."

Hearing their words of praise helps me feel better. Gives me the confidence that I can do this tonight.

"Wear your cute short brown cowboy booties and you're all set," Rylee says.

"You sure?" I smooth a hand down the soft material.

"Yes. You look amazing, Pres," Georgia says.

Poppy bursts into the room with Max on her heels. "Wow. You look pretty, Mom."

"Thanks, baby."

"Now, get going before you chicken out," Joey says.

"You know I do have to wait for Betty to get here, right?"

Rylee gets up and pushes me into the living room. "We will wait for Betty. Now go!"

"Where are you going, Mom?" Poppy asks.

"To dinner with a friend."

She looks around. "But all your friends are here."

"She's going out to the ranch," Joey says.

"Joey!" I hiss. The last thing I want is to tell Poppy that I'm going out with Kade. I don't want to make her think we could have a future together.

I mean, it's one date. I don't need to get ahead of myself.

"You're having dinner at the ranch with a friend," Rylee says so Joey doesn't say anything else.

"If you see Kade, tell him I want to go fishing again."

I press a kiss to the top of her head. "I'll be sure to let him know."

"Now go!" my friends yell behind me.

Stepping into my shoes, I don't put up any further argument. Because no matter how nervous I am for this date, I'm excited.

Because it's another chance with Kade. The man who stole my heart and never gave it back.

Chapter Eighteen

KADE

"Are you going to be okay managing everything tonight?" I ask Reenie.

She cocks a brow at me, pinning me with a fierce look. "You know I've been running this place long before you got here."

"Ouch. It sounds like you don't need me."

"More like I need you to keep fixing it up so we can bring in more guests and I get to keep my job."

"All I'm good for, I see." I laugh.

"Relax, Kade. Everything will be fine. All the guests will be taken care of. Rex has a new menu he's testing out and they are going to love it."

I smile at her. "I know. Rex gave me some extras."

"Trying to woo Presley?"

I ignore her, resisting the urge to flip her off. "I'll see you tomorrow, Reenie."

"Not too early!" she calls out after me.

Grabbing the basket of food from my office, I head out to my truck where everything is waiting. Including Presley.

Stubborn girl as always, I couldn't convince her to let me pick her up. Wanted to come on her own, she said.

Considering this is our first date since in six years, I don't blame her.

"Hey, Presley."

"Hey."

She looks fucking stunning. In a pair of jeans, she's wearing a simple green sweater, cowboy boots, and has her hair falling in waves around her shoulders.

I drink my fill. Her curves. The small lilt to her smile. The sparkle in her blue eyes.

I missed it. I missed it more than I can admit to myself, even now.

"You ready for dinner?" I hold up the basket.

She nods, tucking a loose strand of hair behind her ear. "Yes. But before I forget, Poppy wants you to know she wants to go fishing again."

I laugh. "I'll make it happen. Now, hop in." I open the passenger door of the borrowed truck for the night and get a whiff of her perfume as she settles inside.

It's the same and different all at the same time. That sweetness to her that I wanted to live inside back when we first started dating. Something that lingered on my sweatshirts long after I left town.

Dropping the food in the backseat, I start the truck and steer it down the old worn dirt road toward the fields.

"Where are we going?" Presley asks. Her hands fiddle in her lap.

Reaching over, I drop a hand on top of them. "Figured a picnic would be a good way to reconnect."

"No prying eyes, you mean."

I smile over at her, her blue eyes staring back at me. "You know this town better than I do."

"They will definitely be all over the two of us going out."

"Reenie already is," I say.

The sun is already setting as the mountains come into view once we clear the trees behind us.

"I forgot how much I loved coming out here," Presley says.

"Not a frequent visitor?"

"Not really…"

Not since I left. It hangs between us. This always used to be our place. Presley would come out and visit me while I was working and we'd ride together. Make out. It was the perfect place for two teenagers.

"Here we are."

Pulling the truck to a stop by a small copse of trees, I put it in park and hop out to help Presley. She's already jumping down by the time I get around to her door.

"Can't let me be a gentleman?" I quirk a brow at her.

"I'm used to doing things on my own."

I file that away for later, grabbing her hand and leading her around to the truck bed. Popping the tailgate down, I arrange the blankets and pillows before getting the basket of food.

"I hope you're ready for what Rex made us." I slide up onto the bed and reach a hand down to help Presley up.

"It smells good."

She sits cross-legged across from me as I pull everything out.

Zucchini turkey burgers with buffalo sauce. Sweet potato fries. Chocolate torte for dessert. And two beers.

"Rex is working on a new menu. Experimenting more to hopefully bring in new guests."

Presley grabs a plate and starts dishing out the food. "It

seems like you want to bring the ranch back to its glory days."

I look around at the fields that surround us. "Remember how much we used to love it out here? I want to bring that feeling back. That sense of pride."

"I think you can do it."

I pop a sweet potato fry into my mouth and chew, giving myself a minute. "You sound awfully confident."

She shrugs a shoulder as she takes a bite out of her burger. "If you put your mind to something, you could do it."

I kick my legs out in front of me, settling into one of the pillows. "I could be a slacker. You don't know."

That earns me a laugh. "This coming from the guy who had already earned a dual-enrollment associate's degree by the time he graduated from high school. I doubt you've changed that much."

"I got my MBA early too." I laugh.

"See? You haven't change a bit. Otherwise I don't think you'd be here."

"It's still weird being here without Verne."

"If there was anyone he wanted to turn the ranch over to, it was you. He loved you."

"Now if only I had that confidence in myself. I don't know the first thing about running a ranch."

I've told her I was staying, and maybe if I keep saying it, I'll believe it. I keep waiting for the other shoe to drop. Nothing in my life has been easy. Why would this be now? This night seems to be going well so far, and I don't want to ruin the mood by bringing this up.

"This reminds me of our first date," she says, turning her face to the sky. "Do you remember what you told me?"

I shake my head, not wanting to admit the truth. "No."

"It's silly. Never mind."

Presley waves me off, going back to her dinner.

It's not silly. Because I remember what I said.

I want to be yours, Presley.

I was young and naive then. Thought that nothing could come between the two of us. Turns out, I was wrong.

Is this a second chance for us? I don't want to show my hand just yet. Show her how much she stayed with me while I was gone.

"Come here." I pat my leg and she comes to me, resting her head there. "What do you say we put the past behind us? We both made mistakes, so why not try for a fresh start?"

Presley grasps my hand, playing with my fingers. It sends sparks of electricity shooting through me. Damn. She still affects me. The way she looks at me? It's hard to ignore. "I like that idea."

"You do?"

She nods. "But only if you do something for me."

"What's that?"

"Tell me something new about yourself."

"New?"

"Yes." She snaps her fingers on her free hand. "I'm sure you've done something new since I last saw you."

"I like soccer now."

"Soccer? You always liked watching sports," she says. "Or did you forget about that letter jacket in football I wore in high school?"

"I never actually played though."

"Hmm." She eyes me like she isn't sure whether to accept this as a new fact about me. "I'll allow this for now."

"Good. Then tell me something new about you."

"New?" Presley looks up at me as I run my fingers

through her hair. The stars reflect in her eyes. I forgot how beautiful she is this close up.

"New," I parrot back to her. "If you ask me, I get to ask you."

"I learned how to ride a bike."

"Wait, really?"

She smiles, nodding her head at me. "I figured I'd need to learn because Poppy wanted to learn."

"That's what it took to get you on a bike?" I shake my head. "After all these years, you never let me help you."

"What if I fell?"

"You realize that logic doesn't work because I know you rode horses with me."

"I trust horses more than my own balance."

"I think you didn't want me to teach you," I goad.

She sits up, rocking back onto her knees. "You taught me a lot of other things, Kade."

"Like what?"

"Like…" She trails off, teeth sinking into her bottom lip.

Cupping her cheek, I lean closer. "Like what, Pres?"

"Like what it means to be kissed properly."

"Properly?"

She nods. "A lesson I might need a refresher in."

"You want me to—"

"Kiss me, Kade," she interjects.

The best words I've heard in a long time. I cup her cheek, watching as her eyes widen. Even in the darkness, I can see the want filling them.

I press my lips to the corner of her mouth. She tastes sweet. Like the chocolate torte we had. I sip. I savor. I suck on her bottom lip before I slip my tongue into her mouth. I enjoy every fucking second of this kiss. It's different from the kiss at the diner we shared.

It's slow. The small gasps that leave her mouth stoke the fire inside of me. I relearn everything about her. Presley's fingers dig into my back, urging me on.

Pulling her over me, I groan as she rocks over my lap. My cock hardens. Damn. He can't help his reaction to her. I've always been like this.

Presley King will always elicit this reaction from me. Lust. Want. Desire. Passion.

Everything.

I pull back, whispering against her kiss-swollen lips. "How much time do we have tonight?"

"Not enough." She shakes her head. "I have to get home to relieve the babysitter."

"I wish you could stay longer."

She drags her nose along mine. "Maybe next time."

Next time.

I take it back. Those are the best words I've heard in a long time. Because it's the promise of more. More with Presley.

The woman I gave my heart to years ago and never quite got it back.

Chapter Nineteen

KADE

"You know, things are looking pretty good around here," Sam says.

It's a cold, cloudy day, but it doesn't mean I'm not sweating my balls off inside the barn. With only a few more stalls to finish up, this place is going to be the jewel of the ranch.

Having Georgia here to lead the horse program—taking guests out and helping those horses for therapy—is going to mean good things for us.

I'm just glad she decided to stick around. We didn't have the best meeting that first day. I don't blame her though. She's always been Presley's best friend and is defending her.

At least she's warmed up to me. No side-eyed looks or whispered words. My guess is Presley talked to all of them. Because Joey is the same way now.

I smile to myself. The other night with Presley was everything I never knew I wanted, but definitely needed. Being with her was like a breath of fresh air. Reconnecting with her like that?

It's a new chapter for the two of us. A chance to rewrite our history.

"Hey."

Tossing the bale of hay onto the stack, I wipe the sweat from my brow and turn to look at the woman who, once again, consumes my every thought.

Presley.

Grabbing the bottom of my shirt, I wipe my face off. "Hey."

She holds up a couple of plastic bags. The smell of burgers and fries makes my stomach grumble. "I thought you guys might be hungry."

"Oh, hell, yes." Sam hurries over and grabs one of the bags from her. "I'm starving."

"Glad I came then."

"Did Betty send you?"

She shakes her head. "Nope. I know how hard you've been working to get this place in shape and figured you wouldn't stop for a break."

"That's true," Sam agrees. "He barely stops."

"Hey. Someone has to work around here," I fire back.

"Like I'm not?" Sam flips me off.

"Yeah, yeah. Save some for the rest of us."

"There's plenty," Presley tells me. "I dropped some off at the front desk too."

"Thanks," Sam says. "I'm going to head inside and eat and let you two have some time together."

Way to be subtle.

People are coming in and out of the barn still, so I find a quiet spot for us to eat where we won't be seen. Presley starts pulling burgers and fries out of the bag.

"You heading to work after this?" I ask.

Her Hash 'N Hop uniform shouldn't look so sexy, but it does.

"Coming from work. I have a few hours before I have to get Poppy from school, so I figured I'd come out and see you."

"Couldn't stay away from me?" I ask, sitting next to her and kicking my legs out.

Presley rolls those gorgeous blue eyes at me, passing a plate to me. "Yeah, yeah."

"Hey." I grab her hand before she can get too far. "I'm glad to see you."

"Me too." Her smile is warm and soft. "Now, eat. You'll need your energy for later."

"For later?" I cock a brow at her.

"Stop it." She smacks my leg. "I meant for working around the barn."

"Need I remind you, you did say next time."

"I said *maybe*."

"You're killing me, Pres."

I pop a fry into my mouth, my stomach growling at me.

She side-eyes me. "I think you need to worry more about eating than me."

"I can do two things at once, Pres. I can eat and want you at the same time."

Ever since our date, all I've been able to think about is Presley. How much I want her. How much I need her. *Crave* her.

All I want is Presley. No amount of time is ever going to be enough with her.

"You're zoning out." She snaps her fingers in front of my face.

I smile back at her. "Sorry. You're very distracting."

"Me? Distracting? What, this old pink shirt is doing it for you?"

I hook a finger in the loose buttons and pull her close.

"You could wear a paper bag, Presley, and I would still be distracted by how fucking sexy you are."

A shudder racks her body, one I can feel. My lips ghost over her mouth as a needy moan escapes.

"Kade."

Fuck. I can't contain myself anymore. Not when need and lust drip from her voice. Pushing the food to the side, I pull her into my lap and seal my mouth over hers.

From the clawing hands, she's as desperate as I am. Our tongues clash as we both fight for control. Sliding my hand into her hair, I slow her down.

I want to savor every second of this kiss. From her taste to her soft skin, everything is perfect. I swallow every moan and whimper. Her hips rock over my cock as she grips my hair between her fingers.

"We can't do this here, Pres," I whisper, pulling back and swiping my thumb over her swollen lips.

She sinks her teeth into her bottom lip. "Do you have somewhere we could go?"

"Are you able to stay?" I ask.

"For you?" She nods. "I have all the time in the world."

Fishing the key out of my pocket, I hold it up to her. "Want to go up to my room then?"

Presley steals one last kiss. "Give me a few minutes and I'll meet you up there, okay?"

"Room seventeen. I'll be waiting."

She stands and gathers up our lunch, but before I can let her go far, I grab her hand. "Don't be long."

"I won't keep you waiting, Kade. I've been waiting a long time."

"Not as long as I have."

Almost six years to be exact. Because now I want Presley more than anything.

And fuck, I finally get to have her now.

Chapter Twenty

PRESLEY

My nerves are bubbling up inside of me. Walking through the halls of the lodge doesn't do anything to settle them.

Because of what awaits me at the end.

Kade.

The only thing canceling out my nerves is my want for him. The last time I wanted someone like this was years ago, and that was Kade.

I tried to make things work with Paul. I really did. But the more time we spent together, the further we drifted apart. By the end, we were two strangers passing in the night.

That's something that never happened with Kade. We couldn't keep our hands off each other. It's probably why my dad hated him so much. Didn't see him as good enough for his daughter.

But none of that matters now.

When I came to the ranch today, this isn't what I thought would happen, but I can't say that I mind. I needed a few minutes to clean up before seeing him. To check in with myself that this is what I really want.

Things with Kade were never slow. From the moment we met, it went from zero to sixty in no time flat. We were always together, the two of us.

I've always wanted Kade. I still do. But it doesn't mean the nerves aren't there. Taking a minute to make sure this is what I want helps steel my resolve.

Because I want to be Kade's again more than anything.

Finding room seventeen, I pause, taking one last deep breath before rapping my fist against the door.

When he swings it open, he's still in his white T-shirt and jeans, but now his bare feet stick out. Dirt from the barn clings to the shirt he's wearing. It somehow makes him even sexier.

"Are you going to stand there and look at me?" he asks, a grin cocking the corner of his mouth.

"What can I say?" I take his outstretched hand as he tugs me into the room. "You look awfully sexy right now."

His hand drifts down to cup my ass, pulling me into him. He's already hard as my hands find the strong muscles of his chest.

"You're looking pretty damn sexy yourself, Pres."

His fingers ghost along my jaw and down my neck. Butterflies burst in my chest at the soft touch. It's the promise of more.

I can't hold back anymore. That kiss out at the barn was a tease. All I want is Kade, and I'm not going to deny myself any longer.

Linking my fingers behind his neck, I pull him toward me for a searing kiss. Kade backs me up to the door, hoisting me into his arms.

"Kade," I purr.

"I want to be yours, Presley."

I stop, pushing him back. "I thought you didn't remember?"

His lips trail down my neck, sucking on my throbbing pulse. It feels so damn good, I could burst. "How could I ever forget? Especially now that I get to be yours."

"I've been wanting to hear you say that for so long."

"Probably as long as I've wanted to do this," Kade whispers. "Since the moment I kissed you at the diner. Fuck, I've wanted you every minute since then."

I guide his mouth back to mine. The warmth of his tongue striking mine turns me on in a way I've never felt.

I'm so damn greedy for this man and everything he'll give me. "Then fuck me, Kade. Do it."

That's all he needs to hear. Carrying me over to the bed, he lays me on the soft, buffalo checked duvet and steps back. Lust and desire are written all over his face.

His fingers unbutton my shirt, revealing the soft cotton bra. Nothing overly sexy—I did come from work after all—but Kade is looking at me like he is ready to ravage me.

I can't wait.

Except he doesn't move. He's staring at my heaving chest, eyes not moving from me.

"What are you waiting for?" I ask.

"Enjoying the view from up here." He swipes a finger over my hard nipple poking through my bra. "Deciding what I want to do to you first."

"Do something," I moan.

He covers my body with his, teeth nibbling on my earlobe. "Something? Hmm. What do I want to do to you, Presley?"

He moves down my body, pressing warm, open-mouthed kisses to my chest. His fingers skim the cup of my bra. Goose bumps erupt all over my skin at his gentle touch.

I want Kade to do everything to me. I want him in every way possible.

Grabbing his hand, I try to push it lower, under the band of my jeans, but he pulls it back, pressing a kiss to my soft stomach.

"Not so fast, Pres. I want to enjoy every inch of your body."

"Ugh," I groan, throwing an arm over my eyes.

He trails his hands up and down my sides as he kisses every bit of exposed skin. His thumbs brush over my nipples, and it takes everything I have not to explode.

I haven't been touched like this in God knows how long. The way Kade is worshipping my body?

I want it to last, but want to feel him inside of me right this minute.

Kade trails his mouth back up my stomach before taking one cloth-clad nipple into his mouth.

"Gah!" I shout, shoving my hands through his hair. I hold him to me as he moves from one breast to the other. I'm a squirming mess underneath him as I lock my ankles around his ass. His cock digs into the apex of my thighs.

Before I can tell him what I want, he pulls the cup of my bra down and flicks his tongue over the hard tip.

"I love hearing how undone I make you."

"Kade," I moan, pulling the back of his shirt up to dig my nails into his back, urging him on because I can't take it. I want all the pleasure this man will give me.

"Patience, Pres."

His movements are slow. A suck on one nipple before moving to the other. A swirl of his tongue. He knows exactly what to do to wind me up.

His mouth stays on my breasts as he finally—*finally*—undoes the button and zipper on my jeans. He shimmies them down my legs, before pulling off my shoes and socks, tossing the denim behind him into the pile.

"Someone looks needy," he says, dragging a finger over my underwear.

As he pulls my underwear free, I yank off my top and undo the clasp of my bra. His deep brown eyes rake over me as his tongue darts out to wet his bottom lip.

"Do I get to see you now?" I pop up onto my elbows, locking eyes with him.

Grabbing the back of his shirt, Kade pulls it up and over and drops it into the growing pile of clothes on the floor.

He's even more ripped than I remember, with a six-pack and a smattering of dark hair that covers his chest.

"Like what you see?"

"I'd like it even more if you'd get fully naked."

Kade drags a finger up my leg. It's a tease and torment all in one.

His moves are calculated, undoing the button before slowly unzipping his jeans.

He knows exactly what he's doing. Kade is amping up my own pleasure to the point I could combust just watching the man.

He's *that* sexy.

When he pulls his boxer briefs off, his dick slaps him in the abs.

"Happy?" he asks, giving himself a slow stroke.

"No."

"No? I'm confused," he says.

Standing, I grab him by the biceps and push him down onto the bed. "You've been teasing me and I think it's time I returned the favor."

Dropping to my knees between his spread legs, I take his cock in hand, swiping my thumb through the precum.

"Fuuuuck," he growls.

I drop kisses up the hard length, avoiding the head, before going down the other side. He's big. A lot bigger than I remember. I work him over with my hand and mouth before I finally swirl my tongue around the tip.

His groans and swears spur me on. I take him as far as I can until he bumps the back of my throat. Strong, calloused hands brush the hair out of my face as I look up to lock eyes with him.

"You look so damn beautiful, Pres. Taking my cock like this."

I pull back, wiping my mouth. Because I need more. I want to make him crazy the same way he's been driving me wild. "Fuck my mouth, Kade."

Lust swims in his eyes. "You sure?"

"Yes."

He doesn't say another word as he starts to jack his hips up. He goes slow at first, letting me adjust to his size. But when I do?

Kade unleashes. Having him use my mouth like this? I'm getting wetter and wetter. I could come just like this.

Except Kade doesn't let me, pulling out entirely.

"I am not coming down your throat for the first time." He grabs my elbow and brings my mouth up to his. I cover his hard body with my own.

"Where do you plan on coming?"

He slips a hand between us, drifting down my stomach before pushing two fingers inside of me.

"Here."

"Yes." I throw my head back as he twists and curls his fingers inside me.

"You ready for me?"

"Ready and waiting," I answer.

"Good." Kade stands, licking his fingers as he finds his

wallet on the pile on the floor and pulls out a condom, holding it between two fingers. "I figure safety first."

I nod. "All my tests have been negative and I'm on the pill, but yeah."

I watch as he rips the packet open and rolls it over his cock. I can't wait to have him fill me. Stretch me and make me come and experience long-forgotten pleasure.

He settles over me, resting his elbows on either side of my head. Reaching between us, I take him in hand and line him up as he pushes inside of me.

Kade crushes his mouth to mine, swallowing my gasp. There's the slight sting of pain as he keeps pushing inside until he's fully seated in me.

He sets a hard pace, moving in and out. Fire courses through my body, pushing me closer and closer to going over the edge. Kade's growls hit my ears as sweat sticks to our body at the heat swirling around us.

"I'm so close," I whisper against his mouth.

"Come on, Pres." He hikes my leg up around his hip.

He goes deeper. Harder. Faster.

Just how I like it. And when he reaches between the two of us to strum my clit? That's all it takes to send me careening over the cliff.

"Yes!"

I don't care how loud I am. My shouts echo around the room, and Kade keeps moving as my pussy flutters and pulses around him.

"That's it. I love feeling you come on my cock. So damn good."

He punctuates each word with a kiss before he comes on a roar, throwing his head back. His muscles are stretched taut as his hair flops into his face.

He looks so sexy like this, emptying his release into the condom. He doesn't pull out, but covers my body with his.

Our breathing is labored as I drag my fingers up and down the notches of his spine.

"I could stay here forever," I whisper.

"I wish you could."

Kade eventually pulls off and deals with the condom before coming back to bed. He pulls me into his side as we lazily make out. It's the perfect afternoon.

Until my phone beeps, alerting me I need to leave.

"When can I see you next?" he asks, tossing me my shirt.

"Why don't you come over for dinner after you're done at the ranch tomorrow?"

He hooks a finger into my freshly buttoned shirt. "You got it."

Tying my shoes, I turn to leave, but before I can get far, Kade grabs me and places one long, slow kiss onto my lips. He presses a piece of plastic and metal into my hand.

An old-fashioned room key.

"Come back to me, Pres."

"Always, Kade."

Chapter Twenty-One

KADE

PRESLEY
Do you think you could do me a favor?

KADE
Anything for you

You sure? Don't you want to hear what I'm asking?

You'll always get a yes from me

Aren't you sweet 😊

I need someone to watch Poppy tonight

I work late tonight and the babysitter can only stay until five today

I've haven't ever watched her away from the ranch before

She loves you

You'll just need to feed her and put her to bed

Maybe read a book or two

I know you're taking her riding tomorrow, so if you can't do two days in a row, it's fine

I can check with Georgia

> I think I can manage that

> No need to bother your friends

You're a saint

I haven't gone to the store, so I'll order some pizza for you guys

> I can go to the store and pick something up

> What does she like?

Mac and cheese

But only the blue box kind

> Got it

> I can do this

Trying to convince me or you

> She's my daughter

> How hard can it be?

She'll be easy

You might have to color an endless amount of pictures, but easy

> And then I'll see you after?

I'll see you after 🤍

"Okay, I can do this," I mutter to myself. I mean, it's Poppy. She's my daughter. I can figure this out.

Even though I've never spent any time around kids before in my life. *Ever.* Shifting the brown grocery bag to my other hand, I knock on the door of Presley's apartment.

"Kade!" the voice on the other side shouts. The door swings open and I gaze down at Poppy. "Hi."

"Hi, Poppy."

"Mom said you'd be coming over tonight."

"I hope that's okay," I say, walking inside and shutting the door behind me.

"Yeah. Do you want to color with me?"

I spot her nanny putting books away in her bag. "Give me a minute and then I'm all yours."

"Okay."

"Thanks for covering tonight. I have an exam I have to study for."

"No worries, Becca," I say. "Anything I need to know?"

"Bed time is at eight and she's already picked out the books she wants to read, so you should be all set. Her pajamas are on her bed, and Strawberry is tucked in already."

I smile. "The goose."

"The goose," she repeats. "She can't sleep without it."

"I'm glad we know where it is then."

My sister used to have meltdowns if she didn't have her teddy bear when she was little. I can only imagine it's the same with Poppy.

"If you need anything, I left my number on the counter."

"Thanks. I appreciate it."

I wave her off and shut the door behind her, locking it,

before toeing off my boots and heading to the kitchen table where Poppy has papers and markers spread out.

"What are you working on?"

"It's a picture of me riding Lollipop."

It's a small circle on top of a brown oval. "It looks great."

I lie through my teeth. I mean, that's what you're supposed to do for kids, right? I can't tell one thing from another. But because it's Poppy, I'll tell her anything she does is done well.

"Do you want me to add you?"

"Only if there's room."

"What color do you want to be?" she asks.

"You pick."

She looks at me, concentration written all over her face. "You seem like an orange person."

"Orange? Hmm. I don't think I've ever thought about what color I am."

"Well, you feed Lollipop carrots and those are orange."

I smile at her, passing over the correct marker. "That's sound logic."

Read: the logic of a five-year-old.

"Are you hungry?" I ask. "I got mac and cheese at the store for you."

"Yes. Mac and cheese is my favorite."

I ruffle her hair. "I'll get started on dinner and you can finish your picture."

"Maybe I can make a picture you can take to Lollipop for me. I know yours is in your barn, but she needs one with her."

"I can definitely do that. We can put it in the stall with her."

"She'll love it."

If she doesn't try to eat it.

Poppy tells me all about her day as I boil the noodles and make her dinner. Is this what being a parent is like? Getting to hear about the things she did at school? About her friends?

Emotions overwhelm me at the thought that this can be my life. How? I don't know. Presley and I still need to figure out those details.

Right now, things are good between us. Easy. And I want to keep them that way.

Scooping a big spoonful of cheesy noodles into a bowl, I peel an orange and carry everything over to the table.

"Did I do alright?" I ask, setting everything in front of her before going back to the kitchen to get her a cup of milk.

She stabs her fork into the bowl, pulling it out with two noodles on it.

"Something wrong?" I ask.

"It's not the right kind."

"It's mac and cheese." I look down at the bowl. Did I burn it? It's probably the one thing that even I can make without screwing up.

She shakes her head. "It's too cheesy."

"Too cheesy? But...cheese is in the name."

She looks at me like I'm an idiot. "But this has too much cheese. I like the other kind."

"The other kind?"

Jesus. I sound like a parrot, firing everything she says back at her. Pulling out my phone, I find the text from Presley. There in black and white—blue box only.

Fuck.

"Well, they were out of the kind you like."

I thought I'd be okay getting this kind. I mean, it's cheesy noodles; how different can they be?

She sighs, resting her chin in her hands. "Can I have something else?"

"I'd say pizza, but that has cheese."

"I love pizza!" she exclaims, face excited.

"What kind?"

"Cheese."

"Cheese. You just said this is too cheesy, but you like cheese pizza?"

"Duh."

Right. Because I'm the illogical one in this conversation.

"Can toddlers even eat pizza?" I ask, more to myself.

"Hey!" Poppy pipes up. "I'm five. I'm a big kid."

I throw my hands up in defense. "Sorry."

She hops off the chair and heads into the living room. "Can I watch a movie until dinner gets here?"

"Sure."

She pops into her room and comes out with Strawberry in tow before turning on a show. One where a little girl and boy are teaching Spanish. At least she's watching something educational.

I wanted tonight to go well. What if me screwing up what she likes for dinner means she won't like me? Fuck. I want to be her dad. To have a place in her life.

What if she disowns me before it even happens all because of the wrong brand of fucking mac and cheese?

Way to go, Kade.

I drop down on the couch next to her as we await dinner. Her eyes are focused on the TV, squeezing Strawberry to her.

"What—"

"Shh." She shushes me. "I'm learning Spanish."

Okay then.

Maybe by taking her riding after school tomorrow I

can see if she still likes me. I have access to horses. I'm not above bribery to get her to like me.

By the time the pizza gets here, she's at least talking to me again. And by the time we're finishing her books and she's crawling into bed, she's telling me how excited she is to see Lollipop.

"I'll see you tomorrow, Poppy," I tell her. "Sweet dreams."

"Are you going to tell Strawberry good night?" She holds up her goose. "Mom always kisses her good night."

Grabbing her gently—because I don't want to get on her bad side—I drop a peck on her beak. "Night, Strawberry. Sweet dreams. What does Strawberry even dream about?"

"Playing with me."

"Right."

I tuck the two of them in, pulling her pink comforter up to her chin. Shutting off her light, I head out to the living room and crash on the couch.

Holy shit. I didn't even do that much with her but I'm exhausted. Maybe it's because I worked at the ranch all day, or the sheer fear of screwing shit up with Poppy, but my body sags in relief that I made it through the night.

I have no idea what time it is until the couch shifts next to me.

"Hey."

Stirring awake, I find Presley sitting next to me. "Did I fall asleep?"

"Yeah." She smiles, nodding at me. "How'd tonight go?"

"Eye-opening."

"Yeah? Did you learn anything?"

"Logic doesn't exist with toddlers."

"She's not—"

"I know." I hold up my hand, interrupting her. "I was told she's a big kid because she's five."

She snickers. "I'm sorry she was such a handful."

"I mean, it really wasn't that bad."

"It does mean she likes you." Presley smiles down at me.

"Really?"

She nods. "She pushes back on those she likes."

"Then she must love me after I got us pizza."

"What happened to macaroni?"

"I got the wrong kind." I shake my head. "I thought it would be okay."

"Was she at least excited for tomorrow?"

"She is." I nod. "I got one thing right."

Presley brushes a loose lock of hair out of my face. "I'm glad you got to spend some more time with her on your own."

I stare up into her blue eyes, getting completely lost. We've only been together one time since I've been back, but I already know it won't be enough. No amount of time will ever make up for what we lost, but getting to be with her now? I'll take whatever I can get.

"Think I can convince you to let me stay awhile?" I ask Presley, burrowing into her side. She smells like the diner, but I don't care. I'm exhausted and all I want is to stay right here.

"I'll always let you stay, Kade."

Chapter Twenty-Two

PRESLEY

"Someone's looking awfully happy today."

I startle, nearly dropping the empty plates as I head back into the kitchen as Rylee greets me. "What do you mean?"

"Oh, I don't know. You missed girls' night last night."

"Crap. That was last night?" I grab the towel and wipe my hands off.

"Mm-hmm. But none of us minded," she says, a happy lilt to her tone.

"Really?"

"Only if you tell us where you were."

I can't help the flush that creeps up my cheeks. "I was with Kade."

Time seems to be moving at the speed of a light-year. Ever since he asked me on a date, I want to spend all my time with him. If I'm not going over to the ranch, he's coming over to our place.

After Poppy's bedtime. I don't want to give her any ideas, even if she's loving her time learning to ride out at the ranch.

"Safe to say things are going well?" She waggles her brows at me.

"I don't even know if I should be talking about this." I slap my hands over my cheeks.

"We're your best friends. If you can't talk about it with us, who can you talk about it with?" Rylee says, crossing her arms.

"It's just…it seems too good to be true."

"You mean because he's back in town or you don't know for how long?"

"Both?" I question. "I don't know, Rylee. One minute he was here then the next he was gone, and now he's back. He's trying to have a relationship with both of us, and I just don't know how to feel about it."

"You know, you're allowed to be happy," she says. "I know you've had a lot going on with separating from Paul and the flux with your dad's estate, but you don't have to put your entire life on pause."

"Is it really that obvious?"

"We all see it," Rylee says.

"We all do!" Betty chimes in.

"Thanks, Betty," I yell back, shaking my head at her.

Pinecrest is the gossipiest small town ever. Everyone is in everyone's business. If you look at someone the wrong way, they'll know. I still remember the pitiful looks I got after Kade left. I couldn't go anywhere without people looking at me. I hated it.

"Trust me, Presley. You're allowed to be happy."

"It feels like I can't." There's still too much unsettled. With so much up in the air, it feels like I've been treading water.

"You've been through a lot," Rylee says, dropping her hands on my shoulders. "We all love you. And Poppy, and we only want what's best for you."

"Is starting a relationship with Kade the best thing for me?"

This time, she gives me a smile. "I think it is. I mean, I've only seen him here with you once, but he looks at you like you hung the moon."

"Only the moon?" I laugh.

"Well, maybe the sun and the stars too."

"Okay, ladies, enough yapping. Get back to work," Betty calls out to us. "This food isn't gonna serve itself."

"On it, Betty," Rylee says.

Grabbing the fresh plates of food, I start delivering food to our waiting guests. There's a small group of people waiting. This time of year in Pinecrest, it's always busy. With the leaves changing, it brings everyone here to visit the mountains surrounding the town. It's stunning.

I do my best to focus on everyone, but it's hard. Because my attention keeps turning back to Kade.

Have I really been sabotaging myself and my happiness these last few years? I tried to make it work with Paul. For the first year or two, we were happy. Everything was good between us. Family vacations. Hikes to the mountains. Laughing around the dinner table.

But when my dad got older and he wanted Paul to take over more of the company, things changed. Paul started working longer hours and paying less attention to us. Before I knew it, we were two strangers living together. Things were too far gone to try and repair them, so I left.

Now if I could only get him to sign the damn divorce papers. Maybe then…maybe then I could really have a shot at happiness.

Will it be with Kade? I don't know. He has a life back in Seattle. Every time I think about him staying, I get anxious. That growing feeling of unease never seems to go away. He left once. Could it be just as easy for him to leave again?

Taking a guest's order, I head back to the kitchen to start mixing up a milkshake before delivering it.

"Hi, Presley."

I stop at Serena's booth, giving her a cheery smile.

"Hi, Serena. How are you?"

"Good, as always. You seem to be in better spirits."

"You know what, I am," I say.

"That Lovers card must be working out for you." She gives me a coy smile.

"Anything I can get for you?" I ignore her comment.

Whether it was just the timing or right card, I don't want to admit she's right. Or could have been right.

"Just a coffee today."

By the time I head back to the dining room to deliver it, I smile as I spot two new guests.

"Hey, you two," I say. "What are you doing here? I thought you were riding at the ranch."

Poppy runs up to me, wrapping her arms around my legs.

"Kade said riding horses is always better when you have a milkshake."

"Is that so?" I peer up at Kade.

A small smile flirts across his lips. "I'm pretty sure I told you the same thing back in the day, Pres."

I cover Poppy's ears so she can't hear. "I thought you were doing that so our dates would last longer."

He shrugs a shoulder. "Well, that too."

"Kade, can I pick our flavors?" Poppy asks, spinning in my arms.

"Sure."

"Yes."

I nod toward the kitchen. "Go tell Betty what you want and she'll help you, okay?"

She takes off around the counter and I can hear Betty's squeals of delight when she sees Poppy.

"Poppy is everyone's favorite." Kade laughs.

"She is," I say, stepping closer to him. I want to take him into my arms, but I can't. Not when Poppy could dart around the corner at any moment. "Are you going to be okay with her today?"

"I mean, I think so," Kade says, sliding into a free stool. "Nothing can be worse than screwing up her mac and cheese."

I snort a laugh. "Well, at least now you know what kind she likes."

"It's mac and cheese. It's all the same."

I shake my head, dropping a kiss onto his cheek. "It's not. The blue box is superior."

"Yeah, yeah."

Poppy comes walking around the counter with two large glasses in her hand with straws poking out.

"This one is yours, Kade." She passes it to him.

"What kind is it?" he asks, taking it from her.

"It's a surprise," she says, looking like it's the dumbest question.

"Okay."

Poppy takes a big gulp of hers as Kade takes a sip. His eyes go wide.

"Poppy, what's actually in this?" He sets it down on the counter behind him.

"It's a chocolate and strawberry one. It's Miss Betty's secret flavor. I thought you'd like it."

"Oh, shit," I mutter.

"Is it yucky?" Poppy asks.

"It's okay. I just can't eat strawberries."

Poppy's eyes go wide. "You can't? What's going to happen?"

"It's okay," Kade says, nervously running his hand through his hair.

Hives start to break out on his face. And while I know that's the worst of it, having experienced this in high school, I can already see tears welling in Poppy's eyes.

"What can I get you?" I ask, resting a hand on his shoulder.

"Got any allergy meds?" he asks.

Hives start to break out on his neck as tears streak down Poppy's face.

"Everything okay?" Rylee asks, coming over to us. It seems like all eyes are on us.

"Can you grab some allergy meds from the first aid kit?" I ask.

She nods, heading back into the kitchen as Poppy buries her face into my stomach, tears wetting my shirt.

"I'm sorry," she keeps repeating.

"Hey, come here." Kade holds his arms out to her and she goes. "It's okay. You didn't know, and it's my fault for not thinking to tell you."

"I thought you'd like it," Poppy sniffles.

"Maybe next time we can get something different."

"Really?"

"Really."

Rylee comes back with two pills and a tall glass of water. Kade nods his head in thanks to her.

"Are you going to be okay?" Poppy asks.

Kade pops the pills and swallows them down. "I'll be fine, Poppy."

"Does this mean we don't get to ride horses today?" she asks.

"I'll tell you what," Kade says. "Maybe we can ride

horses after school tomorrow? You mom can bring you to the ranch after school."

"Yeah?" she asks, brushing a tear away.

"Yeah," I say. "And maybe we can have Kade over for dinner tonight."

Her lip quivers as she nods her head.

"I promise, I'll be okay," Kade tries to reassure her. He gives her a smile. "Maybe you can help me make us some mac and cheese?"

"Mom, do we have the good kind?" Poppy asks.

"We do." I nod. I drop down to my daughter's eye level. "Why don't you go ask Miss Betty if we can take some fries home to have with it?"

Her nose screws up. "You always say I have to have veggy-tables with it."

Kade smiles at her misuse of the word. "It's a special night, Pop. I think we can have some fries."

"Okay."

She slides out of Kade's lap and goes back into the kitchen. When she's out of sight, I turn my attention back to Kade.

"Are you sure you'll be okay?"

He nods. "Do you remember the day I had a reaction because you borrowed Georgia's lip gloss before our date and it was strawberry flavored?"

I groan, burying my face in his neck. "God, don't remind me."

"I was fine then, Pres. I'll be fine now."

"At least this will be contained to your face. Not... everywhere else."

"Hey." Kade cups my face and pulls my gaze to his. "That was still a good day."

"Even if you had to have a doctor look at your, you know..." *Dick*, I mouth, not wanting anyone else to hear it.

"Worth it to have you take care of me all night. Even though I didn't need it."

"So you don't need it tonight?" I quirk a brow at him.

He shakes his head. "I definitely need someone to take care of me. Maybe make me some mac and cheese."

I smile at him. "Done."

"And maybe spend the night?"

"Can the ranch spare you?"

He nods. "Yes. They'll be fine."

"Good. I'll finish things up here and take Poppy home and you can meet us there?"

Kade gives me the sweetest smile. One that does funny things to my heart.

"I'll see you soon, Pres."

"See you soon."

I can't wait.

Chapter Twenty-Three

KADE

Things really could be worse. The allergic reaction is mostly gone at this point. It's not the first time it's happened to me—thankfully it's not severe and meds will clear it up. The itchiness on my face is an annoyance. The worst part? Poppy's poor face. It was a gut punch. I know she wanted to surprise me and it didn't go the way she planned.

I don't want her to feel any worse, so pulling open the door to the general store, I'm hoping I can find something for her to lift her spirits.

I mean, what does a five-year-old girl even like?

Pulling out my phone, I call for help.

"Should I be offended you come back to town and I barely see you?" Grace says by way of answer.

"It's not my fault I'm working out at the ranch all day every day."

"That's not what I hear."

"What do you hear?"

Looking around, I make sure there's no one close by to overhear this conversation.

"That you've been spending time with your old flame. Is that why we don't see you?"

I scrub a hand down my face. It's not like Presley and I have been keeping what we have behind closed doors. But we spend a lot of our time out at the ranch.

"So?" Grace asks, pulling me back to her.

"Look, we're feeling this out."

"Feeling it out?" I can feel the eye roll over the phone. "Please, Kade. You've been in love with her since you first met her."

"And she's still separated and getting divorced. I have the ranch and my job to worry about back in Seattle."

"Cop-out."

"I didn't call to get a lecture," I say.

"Then what do you need?"

"What do I get a five-year-old girl?"

"For Poppy?" she asks.

"Yeah."

"What does she like?"

"Well, she loves Lollipop, milkshakes, and a very specific brand of macaroni."

"Easy," Grace says. "Get her a stuffed horse."

Walking up and down the aisles, I find the aisle I need. Right there, front and center, is a brown stuffed horse. "Now that you say it, it seems so easy."

"I'm the best gift giver."

"You're the best. Thanks, sis."

"I know. Now come over for dinner this week before Mom freaks out and thinks you moved again."

I wince. "I deserve that. How about tomorrow night?"

Even if it means not spending the time with Presley.

"Great. We'll see you then."

She ends the call, and I take the stuffed animal to the checkout before heading to Presley's. It's then real life calls.

"Kelly. How are things going out there?" I ask, taking her call.

"Good. How are things at the ranch?"

"Moving along."

"Have you decided what you're going to do?"

Isn't that the million-dollar question? It's one I keep weighing. Things are going well here with Presley and Poppy. But are we in the honeymoon phase? Is it only good because things are easy right now?

There's nothing making it hard and that's what worries me. Back in high school, the first time things got hard, I left. I'm not that same kid. But I also have a life in Seattle.

A well-established life that I need to get back to.

"Kade? Are you still with me?" Kelly asks, breaking my train of thought.

"Sorry, I'm here," I say.

"Contracts are going to be signed next week for the Brissett account. I'm forwarding to you for one last review before signatures. I'll get that on the calendar for you."

"Thanks. I appreciate all you've been doing to help me while I'm out."

"Anything I can do to make this easier for you," she says. "That's all I have right now, unless you need anything else?"

"No. I'll review the contracts soon and let you know. Thanks, Kelly."

"Talk soon."

She ends the call and I stuff the phone in my pocket. Checking both directions, I jog across the street to head up to Presley's apartment, bag in hand.

I hope Poppy will like my surprise.

I don't even have the chance to knock before Poppy is pulling open the front door.

"I saw you coming from across the street."

Her face is still pink from her earlier tears.

"Did you see I have something for you then?"

I hold up the bag as I kick the door shut behind me.

"I have something for you." Poppy hands me a picture.

I'm not quite sure what I'm looking at, but it's bright and colorful. "Thanks, Poppy. I love it. I'll hang it up in my office."

That brightens her face.

Good.

"This is for you."

Poppy unfurls the curled top and pulls out the brown stuffed horse. "It's Lollipop!"

"I hope Strawberry likes her," I say.

"She will." Poppy bounds over to her room, my guess to get Strawberry.

Presley is watching from the kitchen, a smile on her face.

"You didn't have to get her something," Presley says, wrapping me in her arms.

"I know, but I felt bad for her. It wasn't her fault."

"It looks like everything has cleared up."

Her fingers ghost over my cheeks. My eyes close as I lean into her touch. I don't know how I lived without her for so long. Or how I can live without her again.

"I'm fine."

Presley peers over my shoulder before giving me a quick kiss. "I'm glad."

"Is it time to eat?" Poppy asks.

Jumping back from Presley, I knock my knee into the cabinet and wince from pain. Jesus. Today is not my day.

I don't think Poppy saw because she's currently setting up Lollipop and Strawberry on the table to eat with her.

"I've got the good macaroni, broccoli, and fries," Presley says.

"I don't like broccoli," Poppy whines.

"You have to eat a vegetable, Pop."

"But I don't want to."

"You know who likes vegetables?" I interject, grabbing the plates and walking over to the table.

"Who?"

"Lollipop. Carrots are her favorite."

"But that's carrots," Poppy says.

"You need to eat them if you want to ride horses. Get big and strong," I tell her.

She sighs. A long-suffering sigh that only a kid can give you. "I guess."

Poppy stabs a fork into a piece and eats it, a begrudging look on her face.

"At least she's eating her veggies," Presley whispers. "She usually gives me more grief."

I smile at her. "Guess she likes me more."

"You're a likable guy."

I wish I could pull her into my arms and kiss her. But straying eyes from the table might spot us, and I don't want to have to explain to Poppy what our relationship is.

I know Presley isn't ready for that either. But that's okay. Because I'm content with what we have right now.

"Do you want broccoli with your macaroni?" Presley asks, pressing my plate into my hands. "You get the choice."

"There's no strawberries in it," Poppy's voice chimes in.

"Thanks for looking out for me."

I grab both plates and head into the dining room and take a seat next to my daughter. Presley sits on the other side of her.

"Macaroni is my favorite food. I wish we didn't have to eat broccoli."

"Let me guess what you like more." I tap my finger to my chin, chewing my own bite. "Pizza and fish sticks?"

She nods her head. "And milkshakes."

"Milkshakes are good," I confirm.

"What's your favorite food?" Poppy asks. "Mom's is some yucky burger."

"Yucky burger? It's good," Presley defends.

"What burger is yucky?" I ask, taking another bite of mac and cheese.

"She said it was spicy."

"Spicy, huh?" I cock a brow across the table. "Would that happen to be what Rex made?"

"I don't know what you're talking about."

A knowing look is on her face. It's definitely the burgers Rex made us.

"Huh. I guess you'll have to make me some."

"Or maybe you can bring them for me…" she trails off.

I rest my elbows on the table and lean closer. "Does that mean another dinner?"

Presley leans closer. "I guess it does."

"Do I have to eat yucky burgers for dinner?" Poppy asks.

I smile at her. "Only if you want to try them."

She cringes. "I don't like spicy things."

"You'll learn to like them," I say.

She stuffs the last of her fries in her mouth. "I don't fink so."

"Poppy." Presley scolds. "What have I told you about talking with your mouth full?"

She swallows. "Sorry."

"It's okay. Now, finish your broccoli and then you can play before we watch a movie."

"We get to do fun stuff with Kade here."

"I like being here," I say.

And I do. I like getting to spend time with these two. Eating dinner and discussing favorite foods? It's the most mundane of things, but it's something I've been missing.

Life in Seattle was rote. Boring, even.

I would wake up, go to the same coffee shop, head to the office and make a deal, then spend too much time there and not enough time at home. Work was my life.

Pinecrest? There's a balance. Sure, I have a hell of a lot of work to do at the ranch, but I have help. People I can trust over there so I can take some time to be with Presley. Time to try and recapture that magic we once had.

"I'm done. Can we watch a movie now?"

Looking at Poppy, I chuckle when I see there's two stray pieces of broccoli sitting in front of her stuffed animals.

"Poppy. You can't give your veggies to your animals to eat," Presley scolds her.

"That's their dinner."

I reach across her and fork both of them and eat them. "She's done."

Poppy giggles and Presley rolls her eyes. "You're not helping, Kade."

"Thanks," Poppy whispers, giving me a hug before grabbing her toys and running into the living room.

"She likes me, so what can I say?"

"You're cleaning up then," Presley says.

I smile at her. "That I can do."

Presley goes to help her get her movie turned on while I clean up the kitchen. I love getting to watch the two of them together. I hope at some point Poppy and I have a relationship like they do. I think we're on the right track so far, but she doesn't know who I really am. I don't know when Presley will want to tell her, but at least we have this time together.

"Kade, can you sit by me?" Poppy asks, head popping up over the back of the couch.

Squirting the soap into the sink to let the dishes soak, I rinse off my hands and walk over to join them.

"You got it."

She snuggles into my side, putting Lollipop in my lap before her eyes go wide on her goose.

"Wait." Poppy pulls Strawberry back. "Can you hold her?"

"Why couldn't I?"

"Because the milkshake made your face bumpy."

"Strawberry is a goose, so I'm okay." I smile at her.

"Are you sure?"

I nod, grabbing Strawberry to give her a kiss. "See? I'm okay."

I don't think she believes me, so she takes her back. "I'll keep her."

Presley plays the movie and snuggles in with us. Poppy curls into my side with her legs kicked out over Presley. It's a visceral need I have—to keep this.

I don't know how I am going to make this happen, but I need to. I've never needed anything more in my life than these two right here.

It's a thought that carries me through the entire movie, with Poppy laughing and singing along. It's the best sound in the world.

I don't want to lose this. But I don't know how I'm going to keep it.

Chapter Twenty-Four

KADE

"Is she asleep?" Presley asks as I close the bedroom door.

"Yes."

"I thought you'd fall asleep before her."

Linking hands, Presley pulls me across the living room toward her room. A place I haven't been. There's not much in here. A simple gray bedspread and a few pillows are tossed onto the bed. A dresser takes up one side of the room while a closet, filled with clothes spilling out, takes up the other.

"Ignore the mess," Presley says, pushing me down onto the bed. "I wasn't expecting a guest this evening."

"Does that mean you were expecting to come out to the ranch?" I waggle my brows at her.

"I will say, I do like room seventeen…"

"It's a good thing you have a permanent invite."

Presley settles over my lap, my cock hardening at her weight resting against me.

"It's a shame I haven't been able to come over more."

I ghost my fingers over her cheek. "Trust me, I know you're busy. We both are."

"But we're here now."

"We are…" I trail off. "Any ideas on what you want to do?"

"We could color."

"You want to color?"

"Or we could watch a movie," she suggests.

"You want to color or watch a movie?"

She gives me an innocent smile, toying with the buttons on my shirt. "Why, did you have something else in mind?"

I press a kiss to her throbbing pulse on her neck. She smells so fucking delicious, I have to take a deep breath so I don't devour her right on the spot.

"I might. Something a lot more fun."

"What are you thinking?"

Spotting something in the corner, an idea comes to mind. I lift her into my arms and carry her to the full-length mirror.

"Turn around," I whisper in her ear.

Her eyes lock on to mine in the mirror. "Kade," she purrs.

I grab the hem of her shirt and pull it up and over her head. Her chest heaves as her nipples poke through her bra.

"Tell me what you see."

"You. Ready to make me come harder than I ever have in my life."

"That's quite the statement."

I sweep the hair off her shoulder, pressing kisses to her soft skin there.

"I have a feeling you can make it happen, Kade."

"Challenge accepted."

My other hand moves to the front of her pants and

slips under the material of her leggings. She's already wet for me. I'm not surprised. She's always ready and waiting for me.

I unfasten her bra and let it fall to the floor in front of us. I tweak her nipples as I slip two fingers inside of her.

Watching the two of us—as Presley nibbles on her bottom lip with her eyes locked on mine—we look sexy as fuck.

"Kade. I want more."

I bite down on her neck, then lick the sting away. Spinning her around, I kneel before her. I kiss her stomach as I pull her leggings down. A wet spot sits on her underwear and I suction my mouth around it. God, I can't wait to taste her.

"Face the mirror, Pres."

She does as I say and I slip between her legs to lick her folds. From down here, I can see every reaction she's having.

Pleasure is written all over her face as she moans and whimpers with each lick and suck. I strum her clit as she rocks over my mouth. I throw her leg over my shoulder to get a better angle.

"Hold on, Pres."

"Watching you eat me out is hot."

"You taste even better," I say.

"Make me come, Kade." Her eyes are locked on mine.

"Always so greedy."

"When it comes to you? I want everything."

I push three fingers inside of her as I suck down on her clit. I swirl my tongue around the tiny bundle of nerves as she starts to come on my fingers.

I curl them inside her as I work her through her orgasm.

"Kade." She pants my name over and over.

Fuck, yes.

Hearing her reaction to how I make her feel makes my cock punch against the zipper of my jeans. I cannot wait to get inside her.

Pulling back, I wipe her release from my mouth.

"So fucking delicious, Pres." Her gaze is hazy, not quite focused on me. I stand, pulling her back against my front. "You ready for me?"

"Hell, yes."

Stepping back, I start to shed the last of my clothes as I grab a condom and hold it between my teeth as I slide out of my jeans and boxer briefs.

Presley takes the condom and rips the packet open and sheathes me. Her fingers on my hard length make it harder to control myself. They feel so damn good as she continues stroking me.

"I thought you were ready."

Her smile is devious. "I like teasing you."

"I like your hands on me." I step closer, pushing my dick through her fist. "You're not the only one. Now, turn around."

She does as I say and holds on to the mirror. I take a minute to appreciate every single inch of her. Her soft skin. The swell of her breasts. The pink on her cheeks. How she looks at me.

I will never get over that last one. It's the look of love. The way I've always looked at her. Fuck.

I can't wait another second and push inside of her. She's still fluttering from her orgasm and I still.

"Why aren't you moving?" she asks, shifting her hips.

I drag a finger down her arm. "Because I want to appreciate how good you feel."

"Kade…" she whines. "We don't have all night."

"We have all the time in the world." I drag my finger

back up her other arm, trailing a path between her breasts and down her stomach.

"You're killing me."

Locking her hand over mine, Presley moves my hand to her breast and squeezes. Fuck. My cock jumps inside of her. I can't control it anymore. I need to move.

My thrusts are slow and easy. I want to make this last as long as possible. Feel each drag inside of her as she squeezes around me.

It's fucking perfect being with her like this.

"Faster, Bubs."

The only sounds in the room are skin slapping against skin. The sound of breaths as we each build closer and closer to coming.

Sweat clings to my skin as I dig my fingers into her hips.

"Fuck. I'm going to come, Kade."

I'm watching her in the mirror, and her eyes are shut tight and mouth in an O shape. I pump harder. I want to feel her choke my cock as she comes.

It can't come soon enough as I go harder and faster.

"Come on. Fucking come so I can come," I grunt.

"Oh, oh, oh!"

Her moans are quiet as she finally tips over the edge.

"Yesss."

I hold on tight and keep going. Feeling each squeeze of her pussy around me makes my balls draw up tight. I'm so close but want to enjoy the feeling of being inside her a little longer. But I can't stave off the feeling when I come on a quiet roar.

I collapse over her, covering her body with my own. My breathing is labored as I still inside of her. I don't know how each time with her is better than the last. Getting to be with Presley again is heaven on earth.

After pulling out and dealing with the condom, I scoop Presley into my arms and carry her over to the bed. "Can you stay?" she murmurs.

Lying next to her, I pull the comforter over the two of us, relishing that I get to have her in my arms. "I'm not going anywhere, Presley."

"Good. I like having you like this again, Bubs."

"I've missed being here. And hearing you call me that."

"Is it okay?" she asks.

"More than okay."

She burrows close. "Good. I'm hoping one of these days you might actually get to wake up in my bed with me."

"I hope so too. Until then, I'm just going to settle for giving you as many orgasms as I can until I have to leave."

"Oh, yeah?" She rests her chin on my chest, staring up at me.

Her blue eyes are soft.

"You got a problem with that?"

"With you making me feel like I'm flying? No problem whatsoever."

"Good." I press a kiss to her forehead. "Rest up, Presley. You're going to need it because I plan on making you come all night long."

Chapter Twenty-Five

PRESLEY

"Do you really have to work?"

Kade crowds me from behind, his hands brushing the soft skin exposed from where I knotted my shirt up.

Sparks explode inside of me. I want nothing more than to say fuck it to work and be with Kade, but I can't.

"You know I have to."

He groans, resting his forehead on my shoulder. "I miss you, Pres. You didn't come over last night."

"I know." I wiggle against him, feeling him harden beneath me. "Poppy wasn't feeling well."

"Are you sure there isn't anything I can do to help?"

I shake my head, spinning in his arms. "No. She was feeling better this morning."

He smiles, brushing my cheek. "Then how about I bring dinner over tonight?"

"I would not say no to you coming over again."

"Done. I'll make sure to get something everyone will like."

His lips ghost over mine, and it causes every thought to flee my head. I don't know how I ever went so long without Kade.

"Maybe I could spend the night after?" Kade asks.

"You really want to?"

"Presley." His voice is firm. "There is nothing I want more than *you*. I will take you however I can get you."

I look around. The break room is blissfully empty. "Maybe we could…"

"Stop macking on each other!" Betty barks, her head popping into the door. "I don't need my top waitress to show up looking like she was getting frisky back here."

"Hey!" Rylee's voice cuts in. "I thought I was your top waitress."

"Of course you are, dear." She winks at her.

"Fuck," Kade whispers. "Now I'm going to have to go back to work with a raging hard-on."

"You need a minute?" I ask, smiling at him.

"Yes." He shifts as I squirm away from him to grab my bandanna.

Tying my hair up, I adjust my shirt and grab my apron and check pad. When I turn back around, Kade is there, leaning against the wall. Looking effortlessly sexy as he always does.

"What?"

"You really aren't making it easy on me."

His gaze rakes over me. I feel it over every inch of my body. I can't wait to feel him against me later.

"Back at you."

Spinning on my heel, I leave the break room with Kade hot on my tail. Giving him a good sway of my ass to make him feel what I'm feeling.

"Presley," he growls, crowding in behind me.

When we push through the swinging door, a burst of light and noise greet us. And standing there in the doorway to the diner is the very last person I expect to see here.

My mom.

There's one way to kill the buzz.

"What are you doing here?"

Kade stills behind me. There is clearly no love lost between the two of them after all these years.

"Am I not able to see my daughter?"

"I'm working."

I look around, not wanting to draw anyone's attention to this conversation. Being that it's a small town—Pinecrest is exceptionally nosey—all eyes are on the two of us.

She huffs, sliding her designer handbag off her shoulder and sitting in the corner booth. The one right behind Serena. No doubt her ears are primed to hear all the tea.

"Then I will be a paying customer."

"Do you want me to stay?" Kade whispers in my ear.

Turning to face him, I can see how nervous he is. Again, something that isn't unusual when it came to my parents. They never liked him in high school. The boy from the wrong side of town wasn't good enough for their daughter.

"Yes."

"I'll wait at the counter for you."

Tension comes off him in waves. I hate that one of the people I love most in the world feels like this around the people that are supposed to be there for me.

But they are only there for themselves.

"What can I get you?" I sigh, staring my mother down.

"A cup of coffee. Black. You know I don't like cream and sugar."

"I know."

She tells me this like I might have forgotten how she takes her coffee. I walk behind the counter, grabbing a white ceramic mug and pouring her a cup of black brew.

I peek a glance back at Kade, and Rylee is serving him a milkshake. I smile, knowing it doesn't have strawberries in it.

Dropping down across from my mom, I push her mug toward her and watch as she concentrates on me.

I used to do everything in my power to make sure my mother loved me. No matter what I did, it was never good enough. Even when Paul was in the picture, I wasn't doing enough to be a doting wife.

"Why are you here?"

"Is that any way to greet your mother?" she spits. "I raised you better than that, Presley."

I count to five in my head. It's the only way I won't snap at her.

Then I do it again.

One, two, three, four, five.

This time, I don't say anything. I wait for her to broach whatever subject is on her mind, all the while ignoring the eyes I can feel directed to the back of my head.

Serena isn't even trying to hide the way she's looking at us.

This will be all over town within minutes.

Did you see Presley's mom came to the diner?

How did Presley treat her?

Was there yelling?

There will be no yelling if I can help it.

"You cannot keep avoiding your husband." She finally breaks the silence.

"*Ex-husband*," I clarify.

Her gaze narrows. "The divorce isn't final yet."

"Because he won't sign the damn papers!" I hiss, jabbing my finger on the table.

Pressure grows between my eyes. This is a conversation I keep trying to have with Paul, but he won't hear of it.

Because where I am, so is the money.

"You love him. Your father loved him. Isn't that worth something?"

"Does Paul love me?" I fire back, cocking a brow at her.

She bristles under my words.

"Of course he does. He married you."

"That doesn't mean you love someone."

Glancing toward the counter, I seek out Kade, the person I wanted to marry who was ripped away from me. His focus seems trained solely on the milkshake in front of him.

"Presley Ann, you need to grow up. People get married all the time for various reasons. You need to be the wife your husband needs. Your father wanted him to have the company—"

"And never got around to amending his will," I interject. "That's not my fault it is still coming to me."

"Which is why you need to take Paul back. Run it together."

I shake my head. "No."

"Then why are you working here?" Her nose turns up in disgust. "You'll have millions."

"Until the estate is settled, I don't have anything."

"You—"

"I don't want *his* money."

Mom rolls her eyes. "It's not like it's tainted."

"No, but it always came with restrictions. If I didn't behave, Dad would hold it over my head."

Right until the very end.

"And Poppy? Could she use the money?"

I stiffen. Of course she threatens me by using my daughter. I would do anything for her. Which is why I'm working at the diner. To keep her fed and clothed.

"I am doing just fine for the two us."

Again, she looks around with her nose held high in the air as if she's above this place. "Are you?"

I'm done. There is no point in having this conversation with her. It's an endless cycle. Her wanting me to go back to Paul, make amends. Me getting angry. Not speaking for weeks.

Rinse and repeat.

"If Paul really wanted me, he knows where I am. Now, is there anything else you need? I have to get back to work."

She stands and I follow her.

"You don't know what you're doing, Presley. This isn't what your father wanted."

Cutting my gaze to Kade, I find that his eyes are locked on me. It helps to soothe the anger threatening to take over.

"Well, he had plenty of time to fix his will and chose not to do that. And he never knew what I wanted because he never bothered to ask." I wave a hand across from me to show her the exit. "I actually know exactly what I'm doing. I'll see you around."

She leaves in a huff, perfume wafting behind her.

The same overly stuffy scent she's always worn.

"Sage could work well for you, my dear," Serena tells me. "Clear out the negative and bring in better energy for you."

"Right." I ignore her words, walking over to Kade. I don't need to give her any reason to give me a reading at the moment. I don't need to know that the meeting with my mom was a disaster and that the fortunes aren't in my favor.

Or whatever else she might tell me.

"You good?" Kade asks, pulling me between his legs.

I sigh. "I wish things were different with her. She can't see past me not being with Paul and how it's not what my father wanted."

He scoffs, anger lacing the sound. "Does it not matter what you want? Did they ever stop to think about that?"

I wrap my arms around his shoulders and rest my forehead against his. "We wouldn't be in this situation if they did."

"Then I will do my best tonight to make you forget all that."

I kiss him, short and sweet. Because the last thing I want—

"I really need to implement a no macking on the customers rule," Betty moans, dropping off a plate of fries. "Rylee is just as bad when Chase comes in."

"Kade isn't really a customer."

"He's eating. He's a customer. Now, make sure he pays and gives you a good tip." Betty eyes me before turning to Kade. "A real tip. None of this I'll do it in the bedroom nonsense you kids seem to do these days."

"Betty!" I gasp.

"For the shake and fries. And excellent service." Kade pulls out his wallet and drops two twenties on the counter. "Would it help if I leave a five-star review online?"

Betty smiles at him, big and toothy. "Leave a one-star for all I care. I never look at those things. It's a diner. You come here, you know what you're getting. If you don't like a burger, fries, and a shake, go to the steakhouse in Thistle Creek. I don't give a damn. And if you don't like my girls?

Tough shit. I'm not letting any of them go. Even if they have a thing for the guests."

Kade smiles at me.

Betty is right. I know what I'm getting here.

Stability. Kade. Making my own life.

It's nowhere close to where I thought I'd be at the point, but being in Kade's arms?

I'm pretty okay with where I am now.

Chapter Twenty-Six

PRESLEY

"Have you ever ridden into the mountains, Mom?" Poppy asks from her car seat.

"I have."

"Is it fun?"

"You'll love it."

Some of my favorite memories in high school were from going out in the mountains with Kade. Being on a horse with Kade was the best, and now it's something we are doing with Poppy today.

"Do I get to ride Pop today?"

"Pop? Who's that?" I ask, turning down the road to the barn.

"Lollipop. Pop and Pop. It's both of us," she says.

"I like it," I say.

Kade is waiting outside for us, a wide-brimmed cowboy hat sitting on his head. In a dark jacket zipped up and jeans stretching across his thighs, he looks effortlessly sexy.

A smile slips onto my face as Poppy unbuckles herself before jumping out of the truck.

"Hi, Kade. Where's Pop?" she asks as I stroll over.

"Pop?" he asks, kneeling down to her level, tipping up her cowboy hat.

"Lollipop."

"Yeah, Kade, don't you know Pop?" I jest.

"I just told you, Mom."

The sass.

"*Pop* will be very happy to take you up into the mountains today."

She's bouncing up and down. "I can't wait. Can I ride with you?"

"You know, I'm beginning to think you like Kade more than me," I say, grinning down at her.

"What can I say, Pres? Pop here has good taste." He winks at me before leading her into the barn. Our horses are ready for us. Kade swaps out her hat for a helmet, one that clashes with her bright orange jacket.

He checks the strap on her helmet before coming over and handing one to me. "You need one too."

"Really?"

He nods, plopping it on my head and buckling the strap under my chin. "Safety first, Pres."

I roll my eyes at him. "What if I said no?"

"Would you really want to set that example for our daughter? Besides, I want to keep both my girls safe."

His words do funny things to my heart.

I love that we get to spend this time together as a family. Not that Poppy knows the truth about Kade, but being here together, just us?

I could get used to this. Spending afternoons at the ranch together. Riding horses or fishing. It would be perfect.

After leaving town all those years ago, Kade has made Pinecrest home again. Slotted himself so easily into the town and our lives that it'll be hard to see him leave. If that's the plan. It's something we still haven't discussed, but I don't want to burst our happy bubble.

"What's this horse's name?" Poppy asks, breaking me out of my thoughts.

"It's Bordeaux." Kade strokes him on the nose.

"That's a funny name."

"He's named after a kind of wine with his dark brownish-red color."

"That's the stuff Mom likes to drink."

"Way to throw me under the bus, Pop." I tickle her side.

"Hop up, Pres, and I'll make sure your saddle looks good."

Resting my boot in the stirrup, I hoist myself up and on Bordeaux before Kade checks to make sure everything is good.

"Take the reins, Presley."

"You do know I've ridden a horse before, right?" I cock a brow down at him.

"I thought you might need a refresher."

"You sure you don't need one?" I fire back.

"Can I get on yet?" Poppy calls from where she's standing and petting Lollipop.

"Hold on," Kade responds. He shoots a wink my way and squeezes my knee.

He helps Poppy up into the saddle, checks the reins, and gets on behind her. Poppy holds the reins as Kade helps. As we steer the horses out of the barn, the sun greets us.

A few guests are taking off on one of the trails—something that makes me happy to see—as Kade takes us toward an easier one.

Considering it's Poppy's first time out like this, we didn't want anything too hard. I have a feeling once she gets a small taste of this, she's going to want to keep going.

"Pop is trying to eat leaves." Poppy laughs from up ahead. "Can horses eat leaves?"

"She'll be fine," Kade tells her.

Watching the two of them together makes me so damn happy. I shouldn't be surprised that she warmed up to him so quickly, since she never seems to meet a stranger. She loves getting to spend time with him and is always asking when she gets to go visit him at the ranch.

I still don't know what's going to happen between the two of us, but at least I know Poppy is going to have a good relationship with him, which is something I've been thinking a lot about recently.

Kade's life is still in Seattle. Even though he's settling in here, I can't deny that simple fact. I know we'll make whatever relationship work for Poppy. But what if making it work means uprooting our lives and moving to Seattle? Could I do that?

I swallow around the emotion clogging my throat. I've never thought of leaving Pinecrest. Even when everything went down with Paul, it never once crossed my mind. Pinecrest is where I was born and raised. It's home. I don't want to leave. Sure, there's good and bad memories, but that's life.

Since Kade came back, there's been more good it seems. Finally some happy moments after everything had felt too heavy the last few months.

And today, with the three of us out on the trail, climbing higher into the mountains?

It's a damn near perfect moment.

And I want every moment—perfect or imperfect—because I love this man.

It's hard to admit to myself, even now, but I do.

I love him.

Did I ever stop loving him? Even when I was with Paul, I think there might have been some part of my heart that always belonged to him. It's hard to fall in love at fourteen and not be irrevocably changed.

Kade peers back at me and I stare back at him.

"Sorry, did I miss something?"

"Poppy wants to know if Bordeaux wants a carrot when we stop for lunch."

"I think Bordeaux would like that. Do you want to feed him?" I ask.

"Yes," she calls back.

"You good back there?" he asks.

"I'm great."

It's not a lie. Even with my thoughts swirling around my mind, it's hard not to enjoy this day with my favorite people.

Finding a small lake ahead, Kade leads us off the trail and hops off the horse. He ties Lollipop up before helping Poppy down.

I get down and tie Bordeaux up on the tree next to Lollipop. Poppy is already fishing out the carrots from the backpack Kade brought to give the horses a snack.

"She's a natural with them," Kade says.

He drapes an arm around my shoulders as we watch her feed each of them.

"We still need to figure out more permanent lessons for her, you know," I say. "I don't want to keep taking up all your time from the ranch."

"We'll figure it out," he whispers, lips brushing my ear. "There's plenty of time. Besides, she's doing well on Lollipop as it is."

A shudder racks my body. Even the simplest touch from Kade can light my body on fire.

"I should get lunch ready."

There's an immediate loss of Kade's warmth as I dig everything out of the backpack. I spread the plaid blanket out and arrange the sandwiches and fruit for the three of us. Kade sits next to me before Poppy sits across from the two of us.

The sun glitters off the lake, looking like millions of sparkling diamonds. Who needs a diamond when I have Kade Miller looking at me like I am one? It's all I want.

"Do you like my mom?" Poppy asks around a mouthful of banana.

Kade nearly chokes around his own sandwich.

"Poppy, what have I told you about talking with your mouth full?" I chide.

She swallows, wiping her mouth with her hand. "Sorry. But Kade looks like he likes you."

"I do like your Mom," he answers. "She's nice."

"I mean *like* like," she clarifies. "Boone told Carly who told Kalen who told me that he likes Amelia. Wants to marry her at recess next week. Like that."

"Wait, what?" Kade looks at me, confusion written all over his face.

"Boone likes Amelia and wants to marry her."

Kade turns to look at Poppy. "There's not anyone in school that you want to marry, is there? You're too young."

"I'm five." She takes another bite, this time chewing before answering. "I don't like anyone. Boys are silly."

"That's right." Kade lets out a breath.

"But do you like my mom like Boone likes Amelia?"

"Would that be okay if I did?"

A pensive look washes over her face.

Oh God, what if Poppy isn't on board with the idea? I don't want to do anything to upend her life again. Leaving Paul was one thing. And at some point I will have to drop the bomb that Kade is her dad. Throw in me dating him, and I don't know what she'll think.

"I think so. As long as you keep taking us on horse rides."

"Is that it?" Kade asks her.

"And fishing!" She points a finger at him. "I want to go fishing again. Maybe with Mom too."

Kade turns to look at me. "I think I can do that, Pop."

"Then you can like my mom."

"Do I get a say in this?" I ask, popping a banana slice in my mouth.

"Do you like Kade?" Poppy asks. "I like Kade, so you should like Kade."

"Yeah, Pres. You should like me because your daughter does. She has good taste."

I burst out laughing. "I can't with you two."

"It's a good thing you love us."

"I only *like* you."

"That's it?" Kade waggles his brows at me.

"Right now? Yes."

"Can I go stick my feet in the water?" Poppy interrupts.

"Yes, but stay by the shore where we can see you," I say.

"I will."

She runs the few feet to the lake, pulling off her boots and sticking her feet in.

Kade bumps my elbow with his. "You really only like me?"

"What would you say if I *like* like you?"

Kade tucks a piece of hair behind my ear, brushing his fingers down my jaw before cupping my chin in his hands.

"I'd say I *like* like you too."

I press a quick kiss to his lips, not wanting wandering eyes to see.

"Mmm. I like that."

"There will be plenty more where that came from, Pres."

"Good."

Because having this with Kade? This day with the three of us?

I *like* like it.

No, I just love it.

Chapter Twenty-Seven

PRESLEY

"I thought you said Kade was coming with us." Poppy swings her hand in mine as we stroll down Main Street.

It's one of the last days for the farmers' market, and with the day off work, I'm glad that the three of us can spend it together.

"He's going to meet us there. He had some work to do at the ranch."

Poppy looks up at me through her pink, heart-shaped sunglasses. "Do you think he did something fun with Lollipop?"

I smile at her, loving how much she's enamored with the horse. "He said he had something else to do today."

"Kade told me that next week he's going to show me how to brush her."

"And I'm going to."

Poppy startles, spinning around to spot Kade behind us.

"You're here." Poppy throws her arms around him and he lifts her into them with ease.

"I told you I was coming."

In his usual cowboy hat, a dark jacket, and jeans that stretch across his thighs, Kade is the epitome of a cowboy.

Make that one sexy cowboy at the small smile he sends my way. That smile does funny things to my insides.

"The market is fun. Mom lets me spend my allowance however I want."

"However you want?" he asks, sending a wink my way.

It does funny things to my insides. But it pales in comparison to seeing how good Kade is with Poppy. He's a natural. He loves getting to spend this time with her, and I love how easily she's taken to him.

Poppy has talked nonstop about our ride out into the mountains with him. Everything is now all about Kade.

"Miss Serena has pretty bracelets I want to get."

"Serena has a booth at the market?" Kade asks.

"She does." I laugh.

We stop at the crosswalk and he sets her down. Poppy takes his hand and looks up at him. "She tells you good luck things."

Kade eyes me. "Good luck things?"

"She tells you your fortune."

"Yeah, good luck things," Poppy reiterates. "And she has pretty bracelets. Mom said I can spend my money however I want."

"We do have to get veggies for dinner this week first."

"Please not broccoli," Poppy whines.

"Come with me and you can pick what we get."

The light changes as we head toward the town square where the market is held.

"You know, some things haven't changed," Kade says. "This all looks the same as it did when I was last here."

"Be careful." I smile over at him. "They'll still chat your ear off."

Poppy skips ahead of us. It seems everyone in town is here. I smile and wave to my usual customers. Say hi to Poppy's teacher and her husband. Poppy pets all the dogs she sees as we head to our first stop of the day, where our daughter is elbow deep in a basket of carrots, talking with the vendor.

"Hey, Presley."

"Hey, Vilma. How's it going today?"

"Better now that my two favorite customers are here." She gives me a big, toothy smile before turning her attention to the man next to me. "Kade Miller as I live and breathe. I heard you were back in town. How are you?"

"Doing well. It's good to see you, Vilma," Kade says, giving her a peck on the cheek. "Glad to see Vilma's Veggies is still up and running."

"Only place to get a good vegetable anywhere in town."

"Don't let Mr. Moore hear you!" Poppy chimes in, arms stuffed with carrots and zucchini.

"I'll worry about him," Vilma says. "Is this all for you?"

"Throw in a few tomatoes as well," I say.

"Vilma, do you sell to local businesses?" Kade asks.

"Sure do. Why?"

"Any interest in talking to me about supplying the ranch? Our chef was complaining the other day about the quality of produce and I'm thinking I might need to make a change."

Her eyes light up. "I'd love to help you out. Why don't I swing by Monday morning and we can talk."

"Sounds good." He passes over a twenty for our vegetables before I know what he's doing. "I'll see you then."

"Kade. You cannot buy our vegetables," I scold, taking the bag from Vilma and waving goodbye.

"I can do what I want."

I shake my head at him. "Then you have to come over for dinner so I can make something for you."

He tips up his cowboy hat, staring down at me. A promise is written in those brown eyes of his. "Twist my arm, Pres."

Glancing around to make sure Poppy isn't nearby—she's already moved on to the next stall—I hook a finger into Kade's jacket and pull him close, giving him a quick peck. "Consider it a date, Bubs."

He beams back at me as he pulls back and walks to where Poppy is.

"Look. I bought Kade and I bracelets," Poppy says as I walk up to them. "They have horses. Like Lollipop."

"This is a bracelet?" he asks, looking at the flat, plastic slap bracelet.

"Yeah. You do it like this." Poppy hits it on her wrist and it wraps around. "They're fun."

"Put mine on, Pop." Kade lifts his sleeve and holds his wrist out for her to do the same to him.

"Now we're twins," she says, holding her wrist next to Kade's. They both have the same yellow bracelet covered in different-sized horses. "I can't wait to show these to Lollipop."

"She'll love them," Kade says. "Thanks for getting this for me."

"You're welcome. Can we go see Miss Serena?"

I sigh, scanning the market to find her usual booth set up in the corner. Purple fabric hangs from the top of the tent with people gathered underneath.

"Sure."

Her head bobs through the crowd as she makes her way to Serena's stand. Meanwhile, Kade's eyes are still staring at the cheap piece of plastic on his wrist.

"You okay?" I nudge his shoulder with mine.

"No one's ever gotten me anything like this before. It just…it means a lot. Coming from Poppy."

Tears well in his eyes when he turns to face me. I want to wrap him up in my arms and show him just how much he means to me. The fact that he already loves our daughter this much means more than I could ever say to him. All because she thought of him and their time together.

"You've done a good job with her, Pres. She's the best kid."

"She has a lot of you in her too. That adventurous side? That's all you."

"Well, well, well. Isn't this quite the reunion?"

That voice. It dumps a bucket of water over us. Kade stiffens next to me as I turn to face Paul. My ex. Well, hopefully soon-to-be ex.

"What are you doing here?" I bite out.

He holds up a plastic bag in his hand. "Had to get a few things. I'm still allowed to come into town, right?"

Even for a Saturday morning, Paul looks slimy. In dark pants, a sweater, and a peacoat, he looks like he's going for a meal at a steakhouse instead of the farmers' market.

"I've never once seen you here." I cross my arms. Every nerve is standing on end.

Why the hell is Paul here? In all the years we were married, he never once came to the market. It's something Poppy and I do together. Paul thought it was a waste of time to come here for food when we could just go to the store.

Paul smiles at me and I fight the urge to cringe. "I was hoping to bump into you here."

"Why?"

"To talk some sense into you."

Kade takes a step toward him, but I pull him back. "Don't."

"Is he your guard dog now?" Paul nods at Kade. "Your dad never liked him."

"What did you want to talk about?" I ignore his comments. It's no use rehashing the past with him. I want to get away from him before Poppy sees him. He ignores her, not even wanting to talk to her on the phone. I don't want her to feel rejected by the man she thinks is her father.

"Give me the company, Presley. It's in everyone's best interest."

"And if I don't?"

"You know what will happen. Or you can come back to me and we can put all of this behind us. I'm on her birth certificate. I've raised her. That means something here in Pinecrest. I was never absent."

"She's not yours," Kade growls. "No court will ever give you custody of her."

That same sleazy smile gets even bigger on his face. "And yet, it's my name on the birth certificate. I think that will be hard to contest."

"Leave," I spit out. "No one wants you here. You don't want Poppy. I don't want you, so why are you fighting?"

"Because I want what I'm owed. Your father promised me his company, and I'll do whatever it takes to get it. Even if it means feigning interest in a marriage with you."

"Unbelievable."

I can't believe I was married to someone like this. That I tried to make it work. It's clear now, staring back at this man with the slicked back hair and conniving in his eyes that he never loved me. All he wanted was the glory that came with being part of the King family.

Paul closes the gap between us, leaning close to whisper

in my ear. "You know I have the money to fight this, Presley. Do the smart thing and give me the company. It's in your best interest. Then I'll walk away. Divorce papers signed and you'll never hear from me again."

He's gone in a burst of overpowering cologne that I wish I never had to smell again. Fury radiates through every part of me.

"I hate him," I whisper.

"Deep breaths." Kade presses a kiss to the crown of my head. "He won't get Poppy."

"He never loved her. Never loved me. I can't believe I was married to him. Or that he still wants to stay married to me."

"Hey." Kade spins me toward him. "He's a dick. But don't let him get into your head. Let the lawyers figure it out."

"I only wish they'd hurry up because I want to be done with him."

"Is it because there's someone else you'd rather be with?" Kade waggles his brows at me.

With the sun beating down on my back and Kade's warmth on my front, it's hard to hold on to that anger. At least for right now.

"I mean, there's this guy I kind of like."

"He kind of likes you too." He sneaks a kiss before taking my hand in his. He doesn't let go as we draw eyes from everyone in town as we find Poppy sitting with Serena.

"Mom. Look what I'm getting." Poppy's eyes light up as she holds up a gold necklace.

"It's for good luck," Serena says. I'll give her credit—she knows how to talk to her customers. Even the young ones. "If there's something you're wishing for, this would be a good one to have."

"How much is it?" Poppy asks.

Serena eyes her. "For you, Poppy? Ten dollars."

Opening her pink wallet, Poppy counts the bills in her bag before pulling out the right one.

"Thank you."

"Do you want to wear it, or do you want me to wrap it up for you?"

"Can I wear it, please?"

"Yes, Miss Poppy." Her eyes dart to mine then to Kade's. "Hi Kade. I knew I'd be seeing you back here."

"It's nice to see you, Serena."

Kade is polite to her.

"I'm sure everyone is glad to have you back in town."

Serena cuts off the price tag on the necklace and helps secure it around Poppy's neck.

"Thanks, Serena," I say. "It was nice to see you."

"I'll see you next week at the diner."

"As always." I smile brightly at her. "Come on, Pop. Time to head home so you can get ready for your play date."

"Okay. Bye, Kade!"

"Bye, Poppy."

"I've got to get back to the barn and get some work done," Kade tells me. "I wish I could spend the afternoon with you instead."

"I'm not afraid of any hard work." I stand up straighter, tilting my head back to stare into his eyes. "Use me, Kade."

"Use you? You sure you know what you're asking?"

"I do." I nod.

"Then why don't you change and come meet me at the ranch. I'll put you to work, Pres."

A little hard work and getting sweaty with this sexy cowboy? It will definitely put this morning behind me.

I can't wait.

Chapter Twenty-Eight

KADE

"I forgot how much you can get done when you put your mind to it."

Presley wipes a bead of sweat from her brow. Since it's Saturday, I sent the work crew home early once I got back from the farmers' market. It's just the two of us. I would have spent the whole day with Presley and Poppy if she didn't have a play date.

I didn't plan on spending our day like this, demolishing the last wall in the back barn so we can start restructuring it.

But watching Presley swing that hammer?

Fuck, she is so damn sexy, it hurts.

She drops the sledgehammer. "You forgot who destroyed the homecoming float my senior year."

"I should hire you to come out here and do this work. We'd be done already."

Presley walks toward me, a swing in her hips. I rest a hand on her hip as she slides her hands behind my neck.

"For you, Kade? I would gladly come out and work every day."

Closing the distance between the two of us, I capture her lips with mine.

Her fingers dig into the hairs at the nape of my neck. I deepen the kiss, savoring her taste. Hoisting her into my arms, I press her back against the barn wall. When she gasps, I kiss and suck my way up her jaw, nibbling on her earlobe.

I lick my way down her neck and feel her pulse throbbing under my touch.

"Kade. More."

"What do you want, Pres?"

"I want to be yours, Kade."

"Fuck."

Setting her on her feet, I step up. Her gaze is hazy and full of lust. My cock is hard and ready to burst out of my jeans. Rubbing a hand over the denim, I beckon her forward.

"Then take off your shirt."

Deft fingers undo the buttons on her blouse as she drops it onto a bale of hay next to her. Her bra follows. Her nipples are already hard as I cup one before latching on to the other.

"Mmm."

I tug her nipple between my teeth, licking the sting away with my tongue. I turn my ministrations to her other breast, giving it the same attention. Her purrs and moans spur me on.

I drop to my knees and undo her jeans, pulling them down her legs. A wet spot blooms on the front of her red underwear. I run a knuckle over the patch.

"Do you want me, Pres?"

"No, Kade. I *need* you."

Pulling the material to the side, I swipe my tongue over

her clit. She slides her fingers into my hair, tugging on the strands.

"So damn good."

I sink one finger inside of her and curl it. Her grip tightens. I love that I can pull these reactions out of her. I love it.

"Are you going to come for me?"

"I'm so close, Kade. So close. Close, close, close."

I don't even know if she knows what she's saying, but what Presley needs, I give.

I switch my finger and tongue so I can push it inside of her. I devour her, lapping up every drop of her wetness that she gives me.

Tasting her. Savoring her.

No amount of time with Presley will ever be enough. Not when I get her like this. It doesn't take much to get her to explode. I eat up every drop, loving her whispered words that hit my ears.

I lean back onto my heels to look up at her. She looks absolutely ravaged, and I don't even have her naked yet.

"Fuck, you taste so damn good, Pres. I love it."

"Do I get to taste you?" She turns her soft blue eyes to me.

"Fuck, yes." I wave a finger up and down her body. "Get naked."

"Only if you do the same."

Standing, I undo each button on my shirt as Presley shimmies out of her jeans and underwear. Kicking her boots to the side, she stands among the hay.

She looks so fucking hot, completely naked and bare for me. Her tongue darts out, wetting her lips as I strip off my boots, jeans, and boxers.

My dick juts straight out from my body. He's a needy bastard, wanting to get in on the action with Presley.

He'll be happy in a few seconds.

"On your knees."

She does as I say. Watching her below me, licking her lips, makes my dick that much harder. I give it a hard stroke.

"You want it?"

"Yes."

I rub the leaking head over her lips. She opens and sucks the tip inside.

"Fuuuck." I throw my head back as she takes more of me into her mouth.

It's heaven. Warm suction pulls me to the back of her throat. I can't help but pump my hips inside her mouth, watching as she stretches around me. Her hand grasps my base, moving up and down where she can't take me.

It takes everything in me not to explode down her throat. As much as I want to, I pull back.

"I need to fuck you, Presley."

"Do it."

"You ready?" I ask, giving myself a long, slow stroke.

"I've been ready," she eggs me on.

Spreading my shirt out on a bale for her, I lay her down, hair spilling out around her. I pull her ass to the edge of the bale. I waste no time finding a condom in my wallet and sheathing myself before pushing inside of her.

Relief. Sweet, sweet relief at finally being buried inside her.

"Watch."

Clasping the back of her head, I tilt it so she's watching my hips pump in and out of her.

"Look how good you take my cock."

"Like you were made for me."

"Fuck. I love it."

I drop both hands behind her and move fast. Skin slapping skin. Her pussy is pulsing around me. Each squeeze pulls me that much closer to spilling over the edge.

Presley kisses me as I keep moving. Our breaths mix together as Presley digs her heels into my ass to keep me going.

As if I could ever stop.

"Make me come, Kade. Do it."

I growl. Fucking growl. "Let me feel you come all over my cock. Show me how I make you feel."

"Kade."

Her breathing is shallow as her breasts brush against my chest. Reaching one hand between us, I strum her clit. I need to come, but not before Presley does.

"I know you're close. Come on." I grind my jaw together, trying to stave off my own orgasm. "Come on."

"Yes!"

It's all she needs to explode.

"Fuck, yes."

Leaving a bruising grip on her hip, I thrust in and out of her. It doesn't take much for my balls to draw up tight and I'm emptying my release into the condom.

"Fuck!" I shout. Our voices echo around the empty barn as we come down from our highs. The cool air makes the sweat stick to our skin.

Slipping out of her, I tie off the condom and drop it by the bale to deal with later. Presley is splayed out in front of me, a blush creeping up her chest.

Scooping her into my arms, I lay my shirt out on the ground and pull her into my lap.

"Kade. That was…"

"Incredible?" I finish for her.

"Yeah."

"With you, it's always like this for me. So fucking good."

"How can you make me feel like this?"

"Back atcha."

I don't know how long we stay like this, but it's the best afternoon. I don't want to do anything else except take Presley back to the ranch and have my way with her.

And that's exactly what I do.

Because I can. Because the two of us are together.

Now, to figure out a way to make the rest of my life less complicated so I can stay. Presley was right. I keep leaving.

This time? There will be no leaving.

I'm staying for them.

I want a life here with these women.

And I'll do whatever it takes to get it.

Chapter Twenty-Nine

KADE

"Another month of being gone?" Kelly huffs. "Are you really going to be able to take that much time off and jump back in? I know I've been able to manage, but with new deals coming up, we need you in the office."

I scrub a hand through my hair. "I'm doing the best I can here. It's not easy."

"Do you plan on coming back?" Kelly asks.

The million-dollar question.

Do I plan on going home to Seattle?

On the one hand, it'd be a nice influx of cash for the ranch. Something that I desperately need right now.

But leaving Presley and Poppy? I rub my fist over my heart. I don't know if I could take that.

"Send me the final Brissett account documents and I'll look those over." I ignore her question. "I'll give my seal of approval."

"When I didn't hear back from you, I sent them to Jake." Her voice is hesitant.

"What, now I can't even do the one job I'm good at?" I

mutter, more to myself than anyone. "Fine. If there's anything that I do need to do, let me know."

"I'll hopefully see you soon."

She ends the call.

See you soon.

I have no idea when I'll be heading back. It's like I'm between a rock and a hard place. Both parts of my life are pulling at me.

Do I go with what's safe and secure, and leave town again? Or do I keep doing what I've been doing? Stay and show up for the two most important people in my life?

I drop my phone onto my desk, needing to ignore it for a little while. A few of the guests staying with us are heading into the early dinner seating when my voice is shouted from behind me.

"There he is. We've been wandering around looking for you."

Shit. I spaced my mom and Grace coming over to check out the ranch and having dinner here with me.

I spin on my boots, trying not to look like I forgot. "Mom. Grace. I'm glad you're here."

"You forgot, didn't you?" Grace asks, crossing her arms over her chest.

"What? No." Of course they can see through my lie. "I got stuck on a work call."

"Ranch work or Seattle work?" Mom pecks my cheek.

"Seattle work."

"Doesn't matter." She waves me off and hooks her arm through my elbow. "Now, show us what you've been doing."

I give the two of them a tour of the lodge, some of the guest rooms, and take them out to the barn.

"There's still a lot of work to do," I say.

"Kade." Mom turns wide eyes on me. "You should be proud of yourself, Kade. I know Verne would be."

I kick at a rock in the dirt and blow out a breath. Gas lamps light up the trail as night starts to settle in.

"Really? Sometimes I can't help but wonder if he'd hate all these changes we're making. 'Too modern or fussy,' he'd say."

"If he didn't trust you, he wouldn't have left you the ranch," Mom says.

"It's a night and day difference," Grace agrees. "If I didn't have a degree in teaching, I'd come work for you."

"Is this you asking for a job?" I laugh.

"God, no. The last thing I want is to work for you."

"What love from you two." Mom rolls her eyes.

I laugh, draping an arm over my sister's shoulders and heading back toward the lodge.

"C'mon. We have a new tasting menu we're trying out and I want your opinion on it."

"You know I'll never say no to trying new foods." Mom claps her hands, following the two of us.

"And maybe you can finally tell us what's going on with you and Presley," Grace says.

"Is this why you guys wanted to come over?"

"I wanted to see the ranch," Mom says.

"Yes," Grace answers at the same time.

I shake my head, opening the door for them. "You know, I forgot how nosey you can be, sis."

She gives me the smile that only annoying siblings can give you. "You know, if you were more open about things, I wouldn't have to be so nosey."

"Leave your brother alone." Mom swats at her. "Let him keep his business to himself."

"You get to eat tonight." I laugh, pointing at Mom.

"Rude," Grace exclaims. "And to think I helped you choose a gift for Poppy."

"Yeah, yeah."

That's another subject that I'm going to figure out how to broach with them later. Telling them Poppy is my daughter. But considering we haven't even told Poppy that I'm her dad, I can't really tell them anything yet.

Rex greets us in the kitchen, showing us to the back tasting table. Waiters are bustling in and out, delivering trays of food.

It's one thing that people are really liking. Sure, reviews are left on the rooms and the ranch as a whole, but right now? The biggest draw is the food.

Thank God Rex agreed to stay. Without him, I would have had to cut my losses and sell this place off.

He brings over small plates of some new dishes, explaining what they are. I don't know that much about what he's serving—all I know is they are fucking delicious.

"You know, it's a good thing I don't work here because I'd want to eat this all the time." Grace wipes her mouth off, savoring the whipped brie.

"Pretty fucking thankful that I work outside all day to stay in shape."

"As long as you're eating." Mom points her fork at me. "I still say you're too skinny."

"You worry too much, Mom," I say. "I'm fine."

"It's a parent's duty to worry about their child," she huffs.

Her words hit differently than they ever have before. I've only known that Poppy is mine for a little while. And I would do anything for that girl. When I get her in the afternoons, I want to make sure she's safe. Happy, but safe.

I want to ask her if the worrying ever stops. I have a

feeling I know the answer, but it doesn't make me want to ask her any less. Get her best parenting tips.

Whenever we do tell Poppy, and I can finally tell my mom and sister, I know they'll love that little girl as much as I do.

"I'm going to go snag some dessert for us to take home," Grace says.

I smile at her as she scoots out of the booth to go talk to Rex.

Mom aims a pensive look my direction. "You are happier than I've seen you in a long time."

I poke the remaining food on my plate. "Some days yes, some days no."

"Anything I can help with?"

"I just need to figure out things here and back in Seattle."

"I hope Pinecrest wins out. Not that I don't mind Seattle, but I like having you close by."

"I know, Mom."

"It's your life and you don't have to take us into consideration, but it'd be nice to have you home."

"Thanks, Mom."

She finishes her dinner and I walk the two of them out, waving goodbye with the promise to stop by over the weekend for brunch.

These are things I didn't have in Seattle. I would have gone back to the office at this point. Hell, I never would have left.

It's not like I have great balance here, what with all my time spent fixing up the ranch, but I have more of a life here than I ever did in Seattle.

Maybe it's not only about staying and fighting for this thing between me and Presley. Maybe it's also about finding where I'm supposed to be. Until a clear picture comes to me, I feel like I'm stuck in limbo.

With the weight of too many people counting on me, I only hope I make the right choice.

Chapter Thirty

KADE

"The fence along the back forty needs to be completely replaced if you want to keep these cows here," Sam says.

"The entire fence? I was out there yesterday. It was fine. Only needed a few repairs."

He winces. "Sorry, boss, but I don't think you know what it takes to keep them in. We don't want them getting out. Would defeat the purpose of utilizing the back part of the ranch to try and bring in income."

"How much is it going to cost?"

"All of the reserves for the back barn and about an additional five thousand."

"Fuck. Twenty thousand dollars to replace it?"

"It's a lot of fence." Sam nods. "If we don't reinforce it, it's not going to do any good. Especially in the winter when the storms blow through."

"When can we get started on it?"

"I can have my guy out here tomorrow. Barring any setbacks, maybe two, three, weeks of work?"

"And how is that going to delay getting the cattle

here?" I flip through the papers on my desk, trying to see when they're due to arrive.

"About a month."

"Seriously?" I groan, dropping my head to the table. "We can't take many more setbacks."

My brain is already working through where I can wrangle up the money to cover the fence. I didn't want to have to take a loan out or to use everything I had in savings, but I might have to.

I still don't know if I'm keeping this place. Why borrow from the bank if I can make it up later when I sell? But with the remodel taking longer in the guest rooms than I planned, I don't know if I'll have much of a choice.

"What do you want me to do?" Sam asks.

"Get started. I'll figure something out." My phone beeps at me. My two o'clock meeting. "I need to take this."

"Right." He stands, dropping his Stetson on his head. "Let me know if there is anything else I can do to help."

"Thanks."

Dragging my laptop toward me, I turn it on and click into the meeting. Kelly is waiting for me, her cheery face filling the screen.

"Hey, boss."

"Hi, Kelly. How are things out there?"

I brace myself for the answer. Seeing how today is going here at the ranch, I'm holding my breath there isn't a disaster in the making there.

"Great. We have the final paperwork for Raven to sign to become majority shareholder of the Seattle Eleven—"

"She's really going through with that? A women's soccer team?" I laugh to myself, interrupting her. "I didn't think she could make it happen."

"Never bet against her." Kelly points a finger at me through the screen.

"Good. Send the paperwork over to me for one last look and I'll forward it on. At this time next week, Raven will have herself a soccer team."

"Done." She taps away on her keyboard. "You have the initial review of Seattle Corp's assets to review before Triton decides whether they want to buy them out to look over, and if all is well there, I can go ahead and set up a meeting for the executive team."

"Sounds good." I find the document and pull it up.

Seeing these numbers—assets, overhead, losses—these things make sense to me.

How to reinforce a fence to ensure cows stay in? Apparently I don't have the first clue on how to manage that.

"Next week is the final paperwork to sign for the last of the acquisitions before you left, and I think that's everything."

"Damn. Do you even need me?"

"Jake has been helping me out. It's made it a lot easier." Kelly waves me off. "How's the ranch looking?"

Rocking back in my chair, I take in the office around me. I haven't done much in here besides a fresh coat of paint and cleaning everything up. That and a new desk, which I'm sorely regretting after all the new issues that are popping up.

"If it's not one thing, it's another."

She's still typing away on her keyboard. "Anything I can do to help? Do you need new contractors? It looks like there are some in Thistle Creek. Is that close?"

I shake my head. "Not all that far. It's just a matter of cost at this point."

"Remember what you always say when issues come up here?"

I nod. "Focus on one thing at a time."

"That's right. Don't blow things out of proportion and it'll be okay."

"Easier said than done."

A beep goes off on Kelly's end of the screen. "I've got another call. I'll get you the paperwork to review and set the meetings once you look everything over. And if you need help out there, let me know."

"Thanks."

The screen goes blank as the call ends, twisting my insides.

Focus on one thing at a time. Well, the one thing that I need to focus on so we can try and drum up some revenue is going to wipe me out.

When I decided to fix up the ranch—whether to keep or sell, I still don't know—I didn't think it'd be this much of a drain on me.

Verne wasn't keeping up with things, and it seems the further I get into this project, the worse it's turning out to be.

I can barely swing a hammer to save my life. Putting up wallpaper in guest rooms? I don't have the eye to keep it straight, something that Reenie keeps telling me is important to make it aesthetically pleasing.

On top of that, we haven't even worked in the cost of the furniture that has to be replaced.

Fuck.

The office walls start to close in around me. Grabbing my hat, I plop it on my head and walk outside. The cool breeze and sun are exactly what I need right now.

The pine trees rustle as a group of guests wander past. I tip my hat and smile as they go on their nature hike. There's been an uptick in reservations, but with half the lodge under renovation, we're still not making ends meet.

Between repairs, salaries, and everything else, it seems like it'd be easier to set money on fire.

Maybe I'm not cut out to own a ranch. I'm fighting tooth and nail to make things work here because I want to get to know my daughter. But my life is still in Seattle. The part of my life where things are easy.

Maybe Pinecrest and The Lost Spur—and Presley and Poppy—are better off without me.

Chapter Thirty-One

KADE

It's been a stressful few days. Between things going wrong at the ranch and work picking back up, I'm ready for an easy day.

But of course, when running a ranch, there's no such thing as an easy day. Which is why I'm two towns over—in Thistle Creek—buying all the chicken coop wire I can as a temporary fix.

"Do you have any more of this?" I ask the man behind the counter.

"I think I might have some in back." He studies me with a curious eye. "You're not from around here, are you?"

I shake my head. "What gave it away?"

"I haven't seen you around town. And I pretty much know everyone here."

Sounds about right.

"I'm from Pinecrest. I'm working on fixing up the ranch out there."

"The Lost Spur?" he asks.

I nod. "One and the same."

"I heard it was in pretty bad shape. I used to go out there as a kid."

"Well, I'm hoping to get it back to its glory days."

"How's old Verne out there?"

I wince. "He passed away a few months ago."

"I'm sorry to hear that. He was a nice guy. Always kind to me."

"That sounds like him."

Even if he sometimes was a crotchety old man when he wanted to be.

"I'll check in the back and see if we have any more wiring for you."

"I appreciate it."

I grab a few more things I'll need and when I turn to head to the counter, I stop in my tracks.

Fucking Paul.

"Well, well, well. If it isn't the prodigal child."

"What the hell are you doing out here?" I ask.

"What's it matter to you?"

I cross my arms, not wanting to get into it with him, but I can't help the anger boiling through me. Of all the places, how in the world did I bump into him in a tiny hardware store outside of Pinecrest?

"I'd hate for Pinecrest to think their golden boy was cheating on them and coming to another town to get supplies."

I roll my eyes. I don't need to tell him that I already got all of it from every store in Pinecrest. He doesn't need to know anything about me.

"Why are you here at a hardware store? Didn't think you knew what hard work was if it bit you in the ass."

The smarmy smile drops from his face. "I can see why Presley's dad didn't think you were good enough for her.

I'm glad he's not here to see her running around with trash like you."

I grind my teeth together, nearly cracking one of them. *Don't hit him. Don't hit him.*

He's not worth it.

"And she still didn't choose you either."

He scoffs. "If she were smart, she'd come back to me and we could put this whole mess behind us and we'd both get what we want. She never belonged to you."

"She didn't belong to you either. She's her own person."

He takes a step closer to me. "And Poppy?"

"She's mine," I growl.

"Not according to the state of Montana."

Crack.

So much for controlling my temper and not letting this man get to me. My fingers ache as a bruise blooms on Paul's jaw. Shock colors his face.

"You really are the asshole her dad thought you were."

"I'm the asshole? You're the one using *a child* to get what you want."

Paul rubs his jaw, not making a move to retaliate. "You proved why I'm the better choice for her and will always be the better choice. But I don't care about that. Presley knows my terms."

"That's Presley's decision, not mine."

Bitterness laces my voice. I don't know two things about this guy, other than I hate him.

I've hated him ever since the night I was serving cocktails to Pinecrest's elite and her dad announced their engagement. It was a pain like I've never felt. Hearing the woman I love promised to another man.

This man. Someone her dad deemed acceptable.

I fled Pinecrest that night and never looked back.

I really hate this guy. I hate that he got all those years with Poppy and Presley that I can never get back.

"Is everything okay out here?"

The guy comes back out with three more packages of wiring.

"Fine." Paul throws down his basket and leaves the store.

I blow out a breath, scrubbing a hand down my face. My hand is already throbbing from where it connected with Paul.

So much for not telling Presley about this.

"You sure you're okay?"

"Just someone I don't like."

He rings me up and I pass over my credit card, cringing at seeing the total. Another downside to running your own business. You're responsible for everything. And at a ranch? All the little things seem to cost a couple thousand dollars.

"If you need any help with the ranch, or need more supplies, feel free to come on over."

"Thanks, man."

I nod at him as I grab everything and head outside to my SUV. Clicking the fob, I throw everything into the trunk before hopping in.

I can't believe I lost my cool like that. It's not like me. Being around that asshole makes it really hard to think straight.

Something else I can add to the long list of things that aren't going my way this week. I don't know what I'll do if one more thing goes wrong.

I don't know if I'll be able to handle it, let alone my bank account.

Things back home in Seattle really are easy. I mean a

few problems here and there are easy to take care of. Is this a sign that I really should be going back home?

Except…I don't want to leave Presley and Poppy. Every time the three of us are together, it feels like we're a family. I only just got them back. Going back and forth between Seattle and Pinecrest? It's not going to be easy. Sure, closing more deals back home will help with money for the ranch, but the travel will deplete my funds.

At this point, Poppy doesn't even know I'm her father. I don't know when Presley will be ready to tell her, but I want her to know.

I squeeze my hands around the steering wheel, getting ready to leave, but my hand aches.

God, I really wish things were easier here. That we didn't have to deal with Paul, her father's estate, and telling Poppy the truth.

I guess that's life. Nothing is easy.

Especially when it comes to the woman I love.

Chapter Thirty-Two

KADE

"We've only got three guest rooms left," Reenie says. "Seventeen, twenty, and twenty-two."

Leaning against the doorjamb in seventeen, I take in the gutted room. It pains me that we're taking it down to the studs, but it needs to be done.

Presley and I can't keep it for our own secret sex den.

"Things have really turned around here."

The hallway smells of fresh paint and is now well-lit. The windows at each end of the hall let in the bright sunshine.

"I barely recognize the place," Reenie says. "You're done a great job here, Kade."

"I couldn't have done it without you."

She pins me with a fierce look. I have a feeling I know what is going to follow.

"Have you made any decision on if you're staying?"

"That's the million-dollar question."

It's all I've been thinking about. With things picking up at the ranch, we're getting closer and closer to finishing things here. It means I haven't been able to spend as much time with Presley and Poppy.

I miss them. More than I ever thought possible.

"Kade, you have guests," Joey's voice echoes over the radio.

"I'll get the linens ready for our next guests coming in and talk to Rex about the tasting menu for them tonight."

"Thanks, Reenie. I owe you a raise."

"I'll take it." She beams at me.

Jogging down the stairs, I hear the happy voices that help soothe the tension in my aching body.

"Is Max here today?" Poppy asks.

"Sorry, sweetheart. He's with my parents. But maybe you can come over and play with him this weekend. I miss your mom."

"Can we, Mom?" Poppy asks. She's bouncing up and down, in a bright orange coat, jeans, and her ever-present cowboy hat.

"I think we can. I need a wine night."

Presley sounds tired.

Shit. That can't be good. What if it's because of me? She wasn't happy when I told her what I did to Paul, but I apologized. I thought we were okay, but maybe we aren't.

Fuck.

"Hey." I take the last of the stairs down and lean against the front desk. "What are you guys doing here today?"

"Poppy wanted to go for a ride today," Presley says. "I hope it's okay I brought her over."

"Of course is it."

Yeah, something is definitely off. I don't think I've ever seen Presley look so tired.

"I miss Lollipop." Poppy wraps her arms around my leg, peering up at me with sweet blue eyes. "And you."

I smile at her before taking her hand. "Then let's go."

"Yay."

"You guys have fun," Joey calls out after us.

"Is everything okay?" I ask so only Presley can hear.

"I'll tell you later."

She doesn't look at me.

Fuck. That does nothing to soothe the anxiety growing inside of me. It's only because I can tack the horses in my sleep that I'm able to get us ready to go riding.

Poppy is the only one that is chatting away as we follow the trail up to our favorite spot in the mountains. A cold breeze blows through, whipping Presley's hair around her.

I love her so damn much, it's a physical presence inside of me. Why haven't I told her before now? Could that be why she's so off? I don't know, but I'll make a point to tell her when we get to the lake.

The trees are almost barren with winter coming. A few last wildflowers hang on to their roots, trying to suck out the last of their days.

It seems to mimic my mood as we stop and hop off the horses.

"Can I go pick some flowers so we can take them home?"

"Why don't you pick a few extras and we can put them in the lobby?"

Her eyes light up. "Okay!"

I don't know how I ever thought I could leave her. Leave *them*.

With so many projects going on back home, it's going to be hard to leave and tie up loose ends. But I can't imagine *not* coming back here now.

"Pres—"

"The meeting is tomorrow," she cuts me off.

"What?"

My eyes find Poppy, hands overflowing with wild blooms.

"To finalize the estate." When her gaze turns to me, her eyes are filled with tears. "I have no idea what's going to happen, but I got the email this morning that I need to be at the lawyer's office at ten tomorrow."

"Are you okay?" I take her hand in mine, rubbing my thumb over her knuckles.

"No." She shakes her head. "Not even close."

"What can I do to help?" I pull her closer.

"I don't know." She picks a fraying thread in her jeans. "I was expecting another update to say they were still finalizing his assets, but not that it was done."

"Do you know what you're going to do?"

She turns to face me, a watery grimace on her face. "No. I've been worrying all day because I have to do what's best for Poppy, and I just don't know, Kade."

This time, when the tears fall, I pull her into my arms. I find Poppy petting Lollipop, not really paying attention to us.

Good.

I don't want her to see her mom lose it. All because of people that are supposed to love her and never did. I hate this for her. Hate that I can't do anything to help, but have to let her make a decision that could affect all of us.

"It's going to be okay, Pres. I know it."

"I wish I had your faith."

Pulling back, I wipe her tears away. "Whatever you decide, I'll be here."

"You will?"

"Yeah. Just, do what you think is best and I'll be here for you. Both of you."

I hope she doesn't take the company. Because if Paul

tries to take Poppy from her—from us—even if part of the time, I don't know what we'll do.

I've sunk all my money into the ranch. I don't know how I could help pay a lawyer to fight Paul and all his money. All because the fucker wants her dad's company.

And I get Presley's hesitancy. I can't imagine working at the diner is bringing in a lot of money, but to get the money from her father's company? I doubt she'd want to take it over, but I don't know what the logistics of it would be.

The only thing I know is I want to be here with Presley and Poppy. Be a family together. That need to tell her when we were riding is gone. Telling her now will only add to her stress, and I don't want to do that to her.

"I wish we could fast forward to tomorrow and this is all in the past."

"It'll be okay. I know it will."

Maybe if I keep telling myself that, it will happen.

Presley could have a good life for herself and Poppy. Not have to worry about money ever again. My money? It's all tied up in the ranch. If the ranch does well, I'll do well. But until that time, I'm in the red.

I have nothing to offer Presley.

Just like when I was in high school and her dad promised her to Paul.

Poppy is a ball of happiness as she bounds back over, her arms filled with flowers of all kinds. "A lot of them were dead, but I found the good ones."

"They're beautiful, baby," Presley says, pulling her into her arms. "Everyone is going to love them."

"Can I give Lollipop her carrot now so we can put them in the bag?"

"Sure." I pass it over to her and watch as she gives her horse all the attention.

I don't know what is going to happen tomorrow, but I know one thing.

I am going to fight like hell to keep this. My life is no longer in Seattle. It's here with these two. And come hell or high water, it will be the three of us together.

Forever.

Chapter Thirty-Three

PRESLEY

I wish Kade could be with me here today. My nerves are at an all-time high as I sit here and fidget in the lobby of the attorney's office. Everything is settled and we'll get the final details of my dad's estate ironed out.

I'm in my only suit today. The pressed blazer and skirt feel stuffy. I'd rather be in jeans and tennis shoes.

My mom and Paul are sitting across from me. It's an ocean between us. I never thought that it would come to this. My mom sitting with my ex and me all on my own. I got a nod in acknowledgment that I was here and that was it. She hasn't said another word to me.

It's like I don't even know the person who gave birth to me.

It makes me wonder if I was ever happy in my childhood. I never fell in line with what my parents wanted. They wanted me to be a debutante. Be the perfect model child when I'd rather be running around outside playing with my friends.

It wasn't until I met Kade that I got the first glimpse of

what true happiness could be. He showed me the kind of life that the two of us could have together.

He let me be myself and gave me what I always sought after as a child.

"We're ready for you, Mrs. King," the secretary says.

Paul and my mother go first and I trail behind them. No need to make small talk for any longer than necessary. Not that they've made any sort of attempt to talk to me up until this point, but I might as well have been a light fixture on the wall for all the attention they gave me.

I blow out a breath as I take my seat at the table. Papers are sitting in front of me as Dad's attorney greets my mom and Paul.

I get a single head nod.

It's fine. I'm the odd man out here.

My mind keeps going back to our day at the ranch yesterday. Poppy was so happy riding in the mountains, having a picnic lunch together. The fall leaves were blowing around us as we talked about today. Sitting with him, it felt like I was a million miles away because I'm still dealing with my dad's estate.

It hits me. What exactly am I fighting for here?

A company that I'm going to run that I want nothing to do with all to keep Paul from getting it and to try and have some sort of future for my daughter and me? I know money isn't everything, but I thought I was fighting for what was best for us.

What am I even trying to do at this point? Piss off Paul because he was a shit husband?

"Thank you all for coming today. Ms. King made it quite clear that she wasn't going to come back until all matters were settled—"

"So damn difficult," Paul mutters under his breath.

Dick.

"And I'm happy to report that we have everything settled," Mr. Tartt says.

"Finally," I say. "What have we discovered?"

"Presley," Mom snaps. "Show the man some respect. You are acting like a petulant child. I'd expect this of Poppy."

I clasp my hands on the table and straighten my spine. If this is how today is going to go, I don't want to be here a second longer.

"Mr. Tartt, why don't we make this easy for everyone," I start. "What is the value of King Properties?"

"Erm…" He shifts through the stack of papers in front of him, pulling out the right one. "After taking into account the last loan and the investments, net worth as of this year is fifteen million dollars."

Fifteen million.

That's what I get from my father.

"The rest of the estate—the house, the cars, all investments—are left to his wife," Mr. Tartt says.

"Paul, what would you pay for my dad's company?"

"As a married couple, all property would go to the couple."

I ignore the lawyer. "Paul?"

"How much do you want for it?" he asks. There's a hopeful gleam in his eyes.

"One million," I say. "But I want something else more."

"What is it?"

Leaning forward, I drop my elbows to the table. I have him right where I need him. "I want you to sign the damn divorce papers. And when I start the process of taking you off Poppy's birth certificate to list Kade as her father—"

"What?" Mom interrupts.

"I don't want a single issue out of you. I want you to

sign the papers so you will be out of our life. You are not my husband and you are not Poppy's father," I finish, ignoring her.

"Presley, are you saying Paul isn't Poppy's father?"

"Yes." I turn my attention to her. "She's Kade's. I was in love with him, and Dad made damn sure that I never got to be with him. When I found out I was pregnant, Dad didn't know, but he'd already decided Kade wasn't worthy of me and didn't want me to throw my life away on him."

She shakes her head. "Your father would be so disappointed in you."

"He didn't know me. He didn't know what I wanted in life."

"He didn't want this for you. To throw away your life on a man who can't provide for you."

"I don't need anyone to provide for me. I've been doing it for Poppy and myself these last few months. I'll keep doing whatever I need to do for my daughter. Something you never did for me."

She scoffs, shaking her head.

"This is what you want, Presley?" Paul asks.

"Yes. I don't want King Properties. I want to live a life with the man I love and my daughter without having to worry about pleasing others that don't care about me."

"One million dollars. That's all you want?"

"And signing the papers, Paul," I confirm. I'm putting myself and my daughter first. I don't want these people in our lives anymore. Them or their money.

"Done," he says. "You'll have your money and I'll have the company."

"No. I want you to put it in a trust fund for Poppy. She can access it when she's eighteen, and I'll manage it for her. That way she never has to worry about a thing in life."

"Presley Ann King. Why are you throwing away your chance at a future?" Mom asks.

Disdain drips from her voice. I don't even recognize her at this point, but I'm done. If she doesn't want to be in our lives, then I'm done trying to be the perfect daughter that she always wanted.

I want to be someone that my daughter is proud of.

"Because all my choices were taken away from me. You and Dad made all my choices and for once, I'm doing what I want."

I loved Kade and was ready to marry him, but they didn't deem him respectable. Paul was forced on me, and I did what I had to.

But I'm done. I am not going to be that person.

"I am not going to let you control me any longer. I want to be with Kade, Mom," I address her. "If you don't support me, that's fine, but if you side with Paul, you're not going to see me or Poppy ever again."

"This is not the daughter I raised," Mom snaps.

The lawyer's eyes are bouncing back and forth. No doubt he is eating up the drama.

"No, but this is the person I am. So take it or leave it."

She leans back in her chair, not saying another word.

"Mr. Tartt. Please draft the paperwork to make all of this final and send it to me, and I will sign it as soon as I receive it."

"I'll make sure it gets done quickly," Paul says.

At least he's good for something.

Getting the company he wants for a fraction of what it's worth? It's not worth the headache of going back and forth. I've been taking care of us, and as long as Poppy is set, I'll be happy.

"Thank you."

I grab my purse from the chair next to me and leave the office without a look back.

Tension gathers behind my eyes. I've lost my family. They never supported me, but it hurts. All in the hopes that Kade will stay here in Pinecrest.

It's something we haven't talked about. It's always been there—the elephant in the room. He hasn't made a single mention of going back to Seattle. He has a life there, but now he has a daughter here.

And hopefully me.

He told me he'd be out on the ranch all afternoon.

I don't think I'll be settled until I talk to him. Throwing my purse into the front seat of my truck, I rip off my blazer and toss it into the front seat before pulling the pins out of my hair. I already feel more like myself.

I don't know what's going to happen, but at least if I see Kade, I'll feel better. Today is a day of asking for what I want. No, *demanding* it.

I want Kade, Poppy, and me to be a family.

And I will fight like hell to keep what we have.

Chapter Thirty-Four

KADE

Fuck. I forgot how good working on the ranch could feel. How it can work out all the emotions I'm feeling.

Because Presley is meeting with her attorneys today. It's the day they're finally settling her father's estate.

I have no idea what the outcome is going to be, but the anticipation is killing me.

I was ready to tell her I'm staying in Pinecrest yesterday, only for her to drop that bomb on me.

I crack the axe against the tree that's crowding the fence. Taking this down will help with the new one that's being installed now. It'll keep the cows in without any issue.

The vibrations radiate up my arm. I keep thwacking away until I see a truck barreling up the road.

Fuck. Resting the axe on the side of the tree, I wipe my face off and wait. I watch as she turns off the truck and sits and stares at me from where she is on the road.

Come on, Pres. Come to me.

It's like my words call her to me. Presley steps out of her truck in a skirt, untucked blouse and a pair of cowboy boots. Her long hair blows in the wind.

She is fucking perfect. Everything about her. I don't know how I've lived without her for so long. I only hope what she tells me is good news.

As she turns, her eyes lock on mine. Tear tracks stain her cheeks. She shrugs her shoulder and I run to her.

"I…"

"Please tell me you're not going back to him."

She shakes her head. "I couldn't."

"Fuck, Pres. What happened?"

"I gave it to Paul. He wanted the company and all I could think about while I was sitting there is why am I fighting for something I don't want?"

"Really?"

She nods. "I mean, I got some money, but I had him put it in a trust for Poppy. I don't want her to worry about anything, and now we'll be rid of him."

"You will?"

"Yes. He'll sign the divorce papers and won't stand in the way of getting Poppy's birth certificate updated."

"Really?" I can't muster up anything more as emotion clogs my throat. "It'll be my name on it?"

More tears roll down her face. "It always should have been that way. I'm sorry, Kade. I feel like I've messed up so much for the two of you, and I don't want that anymore. I want to tell Poppy the truth."

"Hey. Breathe." I capture her cheeks in my hands and take a deep breath. "You've been through a lot today."

"I have nothing." Her voice cracks. "My mom chose Paul over Poppy and me and I…"

I thread my fingers through her hair. "You have me. You have always had me, Pres."

"You're not leaving? You're not going to sell the ranch and move back to Seattle?"

I shake my head. "No. No more running. Being back here has proven that Pinecrest is where I'm meant to be."

"Good. Because I need you, Kade. More than I've ever needed anyone in my life and that scares me."

"Presley, you're it for me. I don't think I knew what that meant back then. Maybe if I had, I would have stayed to fight for us, but now? I know what it means. It's you, me, and Poppy. And I will do whatever it takes to make sure it's always the three of us."

"I love you, Kade. God, I have always loved you."

"Not nearly as much as I love you." I pepper her face in kisses, kissing away the fresh tears that start falling. "As long as we're together, we can figure anything out. I love you and I love Poppy."

"Thank you."

"For what?" I smile at her, brushing away the tears with my thumbs.

"For loving me. For not running away when you first saw me at the diner."

A snort escapes. "I think I did kind of run away that night."

"But you came back."

"I'll always come back for you, Pres. Always."

Presley pushes up onto her toes, wrapping her arms around my neck, and kisses me. It's wet and messy from the emotions swirling around us. But I don't care. Because the two of us are together. Hoisting her into my arms, I carry her to the truck and pull down the tailgate to rest her on it.

"I need you, Kade. More than I've ever needed anything in my life."

"I know."

Scooting her to the edge, I push her skirt up over her hips. There's no finesse as Presley works to undo my belt buckle and zipper as I pull her underwear off her before sliding into her.

She sighs against me as her fingers tangle in my hair.

"Fuck. I forgot the condom."

"It's okay. All my tests are negative and I'm on the pill."

"You sure? My tests have been negative too."

She nods, pulling me back in for a searing kiss. I guess I have my answer.

Her boots dig into my ass as I pump into her. I rest one hand behind her to give myself better leverage as I kiss the ever-loving hell out of her.

"Make me come, Kade."

I strum her clit with my thumb. Her pussy starts to flutter around me.

"That's it, Pres. Fucking come so I can unload in you."

I keep jacking my hips, dropping my hands onto either side of her.

"Ohh!" Her voice shouts into the wind sweeping around us as she comes undone.

"Yesss," I growl, moving faster.

Fuck. Feeling her orgasm around me pulls my own from me. I throw my head back in relief as I pour everything I have into Presley. She collapses on the back of the truck, pulling me with her.

"Holy shit," she moans.

"So fucking good."

I don't know how long the two of us stay like this before I pull out of her. Seeing my cum spill out from her causes another surge of want to flood my veins. I will never *not* want this woman.

"You want to head back to the ranch?" I ask, sitting up and taking her with me.

"I have to go get Poppy from Joey's."

"Want some company?" I ask. "Maybe get some dinner and watch a movie?"

She smiles, ghosting her fingertips over my skin. "Is this going to be our thing? Dinner and a movie?"

"You got a problem with it?"

I help her off the tailgate as we clean ourselves up as best we can.

"Being with you? There's worse places I could be."

"That's a rave review." I kiss the corner of her mouth.

"It's the only place I want to be. With you."

"Pinecrest is the only place *I* want to be," I reiterate to her. "I'm not going anywhere, Pres."

"Good, Bubs. Because I want you here. We both do."

It's the best words I've ever heard because it means a future with Presley and Poppy. The three of us together. I didn't have what it took six years ago to fight for this future.

Now? I'll do anything to make sure we're a family.

Because loving these two is all I'll ever need.

Chapter Thirty-Five

PRESLEY

"I want to tell Poppy."

"What?"

"I want her to know. Now that everything is settled, I feel like we're in the right place to tell her."

Kade pops up, the sheet slipping down his chest. We're lying together in the same room as always—complete with renovations—having just made love together.

"You're sure?"

I nod.

Divorce papers have already been signed, and the lawyer is currently working on Poppy's birth certificate as we speak. Now that things are settling down, the anxiety about the future is slipping away. Things are set in stone.

The company is no longer mine. Paul is out of the picture. And Kade? Kade is here to stay.

"I've never been more sure of anything in my life," I say. "I want us to be a family. A *real* family. We've been through a lot together, Kade, and I don't want to lose what we have."

"Is it bad I'm nervous to tell her?"

"Do you not want to?" I sit up, covering my chest.

"No, it's just…what if it goes badly?" he asks, voicing his concern.

I smile at him, patting his cheek. "Why don't we take her out on Lollipop and tell her? That might soften the blow."

"She loves that horse more than either one of us."

"At least she's a good horse. But I have a feeling she'll be okay with the news."

Poppy talks nonstop about Kade, the ranch, and her time here. It's why I know it's going to be okay when we break the news to her.

"Then if we're telling each other things, can I show you something?"

"What is it?"

Kade kisses me before hopping out of bed. I miss what he says entirely because I'm too busy ogling his ass.

"Did you hear me?" he asks again.

"Sorry, your ass is a very hard distraction."

"Get dressed, Pres. I'm taking you somewhere."

I don't miss the way Kade's eyes trail over my body as I get out of bed and throw on my clothes, stealing his sweatshirt. It smells like him—the pine and woodsy scent from working outdoors.

I love it.

"Come on."

Linking his fingers with mine, we head down the back stairs and out the door, past the offices as we follow one of the older trails on the ranch.

"I don't think I've ever been out this way."

"I only realized where it leads a few weeks ago. This has been my secret project."

"You have an entire ranch, Kade. Do you really need another project?"

He looks back at me, ducking under a low hanging pine branch. "I have a feeling you'll like this one."

When the trees clear, an old house sits in front of us. The white paint has seen better days, and the black shutters are hanging on by a thread.

"What is this?" I ask.

"You'll see."

The boards of the wraparound porch creak under my feet. "Is it safe for us to be in here?"

Kade pushes open the front door. Dust mites hang in the air. "It's fine."

"Whose place is this?"

"It used to be Verne's," Kade says. "It's mine now."

"Yours?"

I spin on my heel, taking everything in. Old furniture is covered in the living room. A half-wall separates the kitchen and living room. Stairs at the back of the room lead to the second floor, and a hallway in the back no doubt leads to more rooms down here.

"Well, I'm hoping ours."

"Wait, what?"

Kade takes my hand and leads me down the hallway. A wide open room, in good condition, looks out to the mountains at the back of the ranch.

"Look, I know it's not much," Kade says. "But I'm working on it. That day in the office? When you found the old pictures? Verne had plans to fix this place up. I want to bring his vision to life. Make this place ours. There's a few rooms upstairs. Poppy can do whatever she wants in her room, but I've painted it pink for her. There's a great space for a nursery. Even a play room."

"You want to live here with us?" I ask, stunned.

"Only if you want to. I love you, Presley. You and Poppy, and if we're going to tell her I'm her father, I want us to be together. Not me at the ranch and you in town. I want all of us to live here together."

"Wow."

I head back down the hallway, peeking in every room. I take the stairs carefully and find the room that looks the best, ready for our daughter. With three rooms upstairs, we have room to grow.

It's everything I always wanted with Kade.

"Say something, Pres."

"I love it."

"You do?" He stops short of the rickety staircase.

"I mean, it needs a lot of work, but there's room for all of us."

"I—"

"And there's a front porch."

He smiles, wrapping an arm around my waist and pulling me into him. "Did you happen to notice the porch swing?"

I smile at him. "I did."

"I made sure I fixed that up first thing. It's what you always wanted."

"You remembered." Tears well in my eyes as I drop my forehead to his.

This is why I've always loved this man. An offhand comment about what I wanted in life in high school and he still remembered.

"How could I ever forget? We always talked about reading to our kids on the swing. Then I'd put them to sleep while you got to rest and then I'd come back and rub your feet."

"It's perfect, Kade. I can't believe you're going to do this for us."

"I would give you anything you ask for."

"I want the moon."

He laughs. "Within reason. But I'll paint you a moon wherever you want it in here."

"I love you, Bubs."

"We might have to change that Bubs to hubs soon."

I kiss him. One that is so full of love, it's threatening to burst out of me. "One thing at a time, okay? Let's get settled here with Poppy and then we'll cross that bridge."

"You want to get married, right?" he asks.

"Yes. But why don't we let the ink dry on my divorce papers first."

"Okay," he sighs. "But make no mistake, I will be popping the question to you."

"You better. Because I want to marry you and fill this house with kids."

"That sounds like a great plan."

One that I can't wait to put into action. Because I'm finally getting the life I always wanted with Kade. A house, a couple of kids, and him.

What more could a girl ever need?

Chapter Thirty-Six

PRESLEY

"Where are we going?" Poppy's head is on a swivel in the backseat. "We've never ridden here before."

"It's a surprise," Kade tells her.

His hand squeezes my knee. I know he's anxious today. Not only are we going to show Poppy the house we'll be moving into, but we'll be telling her the news that Kade is her father.

She loves Kade. She's always asking to go see him. To go play and ride at the ranch. I think it will go well, but you never know.

"I like surprises."

"Well, we're here," Kade says.

The house seems brighter today. Maybe it's because I know what it now holds for all of us or the hope that it's the first day that we'll all be a family.

"It's a house," Poppy states matter-of-factly as I help her out of the truck before her eyes spot a tire swing hanging from the large oak tree out front. "Can I go swing?"

"In a minute," I say. "Come see the house first."

Taking her hand, Kade and I lead her inside. The kitchen is well underway—the cabinets are painted and new appliances are waiting to be installed. Piles of wood are stacked in the corner that will make up the new floors. He doesn't waste any time. It's one of the reasons I love him.

That and the fact that he's staying. I never thought I'd get this in my life, but we're here. And it couldn't be better.

"It's not very pretty," Poppy says.

"Well, I'm hoping that it'll be pretty when I move in."

"Are you staying here?"

"Would that be okay with you?" Kade asks, nodding his head.

"Yeah."

"Good." Kade smiles. "Why don't we show you the upstairs?"

"Okay." She shrugs a shoulder. She doesn't know why we're here, but it'll make sense later.

Kade has already painted Poppy's room. Her eyes are taking everything in. With three rooms up here, she'll have another room for all the toys that Kade is going to no doubt shower her with.

"Can we go outside to the swing?" Poppy asks as we head back downstairs.

"Sure, baby."

The porch swing is my favorite part of the house. "Will I get to come over and play in the yard and swing on the swing?"

Dropping down, I beckon Poppy over.

"Sweetheart, can we talk to you?"

She bounds over, scooting into my lap on the porch swing, Strawberry and her stuffed Lollipop in tow. "Am I in trouble?"

I brush a blonde strand of hair out of her face. "No, but we have something to tell you."

Kade's leg is shaking next to mine. I know he's nervous. We've been talking about this for a while now. There's no easy way to tell Poppy the person she thought was her dad isn't actually her dad, but instead it's the guy who's been hanging around all the time.

"There is no easy way to say this, Poppy, but Kade is your dad."

"What about my daddy?" she asks, looking confused.

I squeeze her closer. "Kade is your dad. He didn't know, so we said Paul was your dad to make it less confusing. I'm sorry, sweetheart, and I know this might be hard because he's no longer around—"

"Kade is my dad?" she asks, interrupting me.

"I am," Kade says. "I hope that's okay, because I really love you, Poppy, and I'd like to stay here with you and your mom."

"Be a family?"

"Yes," I say. "And this house? If you want, we can live here with Kade."

Poppy looks between the two of us. I can see the questions forming in her head. The first one she asks?

"Will I get a baby brother or sister?"

Kade nearly chokes next to me, coughing to cover it up.

"Poppy, do you know what we told you?" I ask, wondering if she got the message.

"Kade's my dad. I love Kade and I think you love him," she starts, "and Margot said her parents love each other and she got a baby sister. So do I get one?"

Out of the corner of my eye, I see Kade fighting a smile.

"Do you want a baby brother or sister?" he asks.

"Yes." She nods. "I want someone to play with."

"Think we can do that, Pres?" Kade asks, turning his attention to me.

"One thing at a time. Why don't we get settled here and then we'll revisit that conversation."

"Yes." Poppy pumps her fist before hugging Kade. "I'm glad you're my dad. Can I go swing now?"

"Of course, Pop," he says.

She runs off into the yard toward the tire swing hanging in the tree. Her excited shouts reach our ears as she kicks off the ground.

Tears well in Kade's eyes when I face him. "That went better than I thought. I thought she'd hate me because I missed out on so much of her life."

"That's my fault. She might have more questions when she's older, but it's easy to see she loves you, Kade. We both do."

Kade pulls me in for a hug. "Not as much as I love you two. Maybe that's why Verne left me the ranch. To bring me back here to realize this was where I'm meant to be."

I brush my fingers over his cheeks, pushing the strands of hair out of his eyes. "I have no doubt he and Arlene were up there causing mischief together to make this happen."

"You know, I really do like her idea of giving her a brother and sister."

"Kade." I smack him on the chest. "You have to get the ranch ready, and this house still isn't livable."

"Doesn't mean we can't practice."

I cover his mouth with my hand. "Later. We can't discuss that with Poppy around."

He pulls my hand down. "You heard her. She loves me and thinks you love me, so why not? It's not like we'll be getting a baby tomorrow."

"You're incorrigible."

"What can I say? I think I love you."

I smile at him. "I think I love you too."

He kisses me. It's soft and sweet. The promise of our life together. A life that is going to get better. One that will have its hard times, but it won't matter. We'll get through everything. Because we'll be together.

Just how it should be.

Kade, Poppy, and me. Our family. This ranch here in Pinecrest. It's going to be our lives. Back in high school, it's all I ever wanted. My dream.

Now? Now, my dream is finally coming true.

I can't wait.

Epilogue

SAM - FOUR MONTHS LATER

"This place looks amazing."

Kade claps me on the back. "I couldn't have done it without you."

"I'm glad you decided to stay. The Lost Spur wouldn't be the same without you."

Looking around the barn, it's ready for our big day to celebrate all the renovations being complete. Lights are strung up and all the stalls are freshly mucked so guests can come out and see the horses and go for a ride.

In all the years I've worked here, it's never looked this good.

"Come on. Let's head up to the lodge."

I follow Kade, my eyes admiring everything that's been done. Even the trails look better. By the time we get back to the main building, crowds of people have already gathered. The ranch is the place to be in Pinecrest today.

And it seems the entire town has come out for the big day.

A few of the newer workers are showing people

around. Updates on the cabins. The lodge entirely redone. A brand-new menu that people can try today.

Heading inside to grab a drink and mingle, my eyes immediately find our front desk manager.

Joey Andrews.

The woman is so damn beautiful, it hurts to look at her. When she spots me, her face lights up.

"Hey, Sam. How are things out at the barn?"

I drop my arms on the counter and lean closer to her. "Ready to go. Horses are freshly groomed and ready to ride."

"Guests will love seeing the trails in the spring," she says. "Poppy has been talking non-stop about going out today."

I smile at her. "Kade said he was taking her out later today once everyone cleared out."

"And you? Do you plan on going riding?"

"I'll be taking some guests on the cattle drives later."

Joey leans closer. There's a sparkle in her deep brown eyes. A playful glint that I can't help but focus on. "They'll be lucky to have you as their guide."

"Maybe I can take you out sometime."

"I'd like that. Show me the ropes."

There's a hint, a tease, in her voice.

"You got it." I rap my knuckles against the counter, putting distance between the two of us. "I need to get up to the dining room for Kade's toast."

Joey walks around the desk. "I'll come with you."

"Great."

Not great.

The very last thing I need is to surround myself with this woman. This woman that I can't stop thinking about but is twenty years my junior.

I do my best to ignore the heat that zings through me

when her elbow brushes against mine. Or how damn good she smells.

The sweet smell of her perfume shouldn't be so damn enticing, but it is.

"Can I get you something to drink?" I ask.

At least this will put some space between the two of us.

"That'd be great. I'll take a glass of white wine."

"You got it." I wink at her.

Fuck. Rein it in, Sam.

A bar is set up in the back corner of the dining room. The regular tables were replaced with high-top ones. Apps and desserts are carried around by the servers.

Everything in here smells amazing.

The kitchen staff did a soft opening the other night, and I know guests will devour everything on the menu. It's fucking delicious.

I order an old-fashioned for myself and wine for Joey. The bartender mixes my drink and pours a healthy serving for Joey. She gives me a wide, happy smile as I head back over to her. Before I can escape her presence, Kade's voice calls everyone's attention to him.

"I want to thank everyone for being here today," Kade starts. "Fixing up The Lost Spur was no easy feat."

Presley and Poppy are by his side. They are the epitome of a loving, happy family. Something I haven't had in a long time. Too damn long.

I'd be jealous if it were anyone else but Kade. He deserves it after all these two have been through.

"We wouldn't be standing here today if it weren't for all of you. Because of your hard work, we were able to restore this place to her former glory. I can't wait for guests, old and new, to experience what we already know. How special this place is."

Claps and cheers ring throughout the dining room.

"If you could raise your glass," Kade says. "I'd like to toast all of you. Everyone who helped, and most importantly, Verne. Thanks for giving us this place that we can all be proud of."

"To Verne!" everyone echoes.

I clink my glass against Joey's and take a sip of my drink. Fuck, that's good.

"I'm going to go say hi to Presley." Joey nudges me with her elbow. "I'll see you around."

"Yeah, see you around."

I take another sip, watching her as she goes.

The skirt she's wearing highlights her voluptuous ass. The shirt—complete with the ranch logo—stretches across her chest.

Joey has no right to make the uniform look that good.

Various people come up and congratulate me on the grand reopening. They all know I'll be managing the barn and the ranching side of things here.

It's something I'm excited for. Having moved around a lot before settling back down here, I'm ready for the responsibility of it.

"If it isn't Sam Shaw."

I turn to see my best friend coming my way, taking his extended hand. "Greg. Nice to see you."

"It's been a minute," he says. "If only I could pull you away from the ranch for our poker nights."

"Maybe now that this place is open, I'll be able to come around more."

"Good. We miss you around town."

I look around the dining room, loving how good it looks. Kade and I painstakingly redid the two-story fireplace. We placed each stone by hand. It was a bitch, but it looks incredible.

"When's the next time that you're playing?"

"Next weekend," he says.

"I'll be there."

"Good. Now, I'm going to go find that daughter of mine and get a tour of this place."

"Enjoy." I shake his hand as he leaves. "I'll see you around."

I stroll and mingle, making small talk and greeting guests. Words of praise are heaped on me as I thank people for joining us.

As I move around the room, my eyes keep drifting back toward the woman that I can't stop thinking about. The one I *shouldn't* be thinking about. Because she's now hugging her dad.

My best friend.

I am so completely gone for my best friend's daughter. If her dad knew, I'd be dead and buried where no one could find me.

Joey Andrews is completely off-limits.

If only I could get all of me on board with that.

Keep reading for more Kade, Presley, and Poppy…

Bonus Scene

KADE - TEN YEARS LATER

"Would you stop looking out the window?" Presley chides. "She'll be home in a few minutes."

"Her curfew was ten minutes ago."

"Kade." Presley's voice is firm. "It's only nine. She's fine."

I peer back at her where she's sitting on the couch. Liam is asleep next to her. He's wrapped up in his blanket with his stuffie sticking out.

"Do you remember what we did on our first date?"

She smiles at me. "We made out in your car until midnight. I'm pretty sure Poppy won't be doing that."

"Why not?" I stand, letting the curtain fall back into place.

"Because she's not out to piss off her parents like I was by breaking curfew."

I smile down at her before stealing a sweet kiss. "Pissing them off or not, we did have fun."

"Mmm," she purrs. "We did."

"You want to go out on a date with me, Pres?"

"With you, hubs? Yeah, I do."

"Good. Grace is coming over tomorrow night to watch the kids."

"You know Poppy doesn't need a babysitter."

I nod. "I know, but sometimes it's easier to have Grace here to help cook."

Presley shakes her head. "I really have failed Poppy."

"I don't think anyone will say that."

"I'm serious." She smacks me in the chest. "She'll be going off to college soon and what if she can't survive because she can't cook?"

"She makes a mean mac and cheese." I smile at her. "But can we also not talk about our daughter going to college? It's too soon."

"It'll be here before you know it."

I peer over at our son. He is the spitting image of me. "At least we still have Liam. Maybe I can convince him to never leave us."

Presley runs her fingers through my hair, pressing a kiss to my forehead. "They'll leave and you and I will be just fine. Besides, you know they'll always come home and then we'll be ready to kick them out."

"I don't know if that'll happen."

Even the thought of the two of them going off to college makes my heart break. I love my family more than anything, and I can't stand the thought of our kids leaving us. Presley is way too okay with it. But knowing her, she's putting on a front. She'll be a blubbering mess just like me when we drop Poppy off at college.

Maybe I can convince her to stay in state so she'll be close by. Or go to school online. The ranch is booming and she's one of my best instructors. I should pitch that idea to her. Even if Presley would castrate me for suggesting it.

Liam shifts, rolling over toward the back of the couch. "We should put him to bed."

"I'll take him up."

Lifting Liam into my arms, I carry him upstairs and tuck him into his race car bed. Kid loves his cars. Maybe one day I'll learn how to fix up a car with him. We still have Verne's old tan car in the spare garage. I can't bring myself to part with it.

By the time I'm coming back downstairs, I hear Poppy's voice. She's sitting on the couch with her mom, chatting about her night—I'm guessing.

"How was the big date?" I ask, grabbing a beer from the fridge and walking into the living room.

"Daaaad." She rolls her eyes.

"What? I'm not allowed to ask?"

"You're lucky he wasn't waiting outside," Presley says.

"Oh my God, Dad!" Poppy looks exasperated.

"What? I wasn't." I throw my hands up in defense.

"Were you looking out the window?"

She pins me with a look that is so much like Presley's it knocks me on my ass.

"Oh my God! You totally were."

"So sue me." I drop down onto the couch on the other side of Presley. "It's your first date."

"I'm surprised you didn't scare him off," Poppy says. "You know that Kyle is a very nice guy."

I shake my head, sipping my beer. I was a nice guy in high school and I know what Presley and I got up to.

"You'll have to forgive your dad," Presley says, patting my knee. "He is having some big feelings about both of you growing up."

"You realize Liam is six, right? His favorite thing to do is go out on the ranch and chase the cows."

I smile. "At least I still have one kid."

"Was he like this all night?" Poppy asks her mom.

"No."

"Yes."

We answer at the same time.

"Way to call me out, Pres," I scoff.

"You need to chill, Dad. Kyle is taking me out next weekend."

"Where are you going?" I ask her.

"We're getting pancakes after studying for our history final."

I eye her. "Maybe next time we can take you."

Presley elbows me in the side. She knows exactly what I'm doing. I guess nine years of marriage means you know what the other person is thinking.

"As long as you promise not to embarrass me," she says.

"When have I ever embarrassed you?" I ask.

"Do you want her to answer that?" Presley asks as Poppy breaks out into laughter.

"Ouch. What a rough crowd tonight."

"Love you, Dad." Poppy drops a kiss on my cheek before darting upstairs. "Love you, Mom."

"Love you, Pop. Don't forget you're teaching riding lessons tomorrow."

"I know," she calls out.

Presley turns on the TV, stealing my beer and grabbing a sip. "I think I'll take Poppy on her date."

"Are you going to be more *chill*?" I laugh.

"You are being a bit over the top, Kade."

"I'm allowed to worry about our children."

"There's worry and then there's scaring off Poppy's first boyfriend."

I groan. "I don't like her dating."

"And if it were up to you, she wouldn't date until she was thirty."

"Maybe even forty."

Presley throws a leg over my lap and settles over me. Her blue eyes are full of love as they stare down at me. "What am I going to do with you, Kade Miller?"

"Mmm. I don't know, Mrs. Miller. I have some ideas if you need them."

"Maybe a good make out session in the old car will make you feel better."

"We are definitely going to be doing that. But how about I take you upstairs and we do all the things we wanted to on our first date?"

Presley twirls her fingers through the hair at the nape of my neck. "Who said I wanted to do that?"

"Ouch. Really rough crowd tonight."

"More like the second date."

I capture her lips with mine. I will never get tired of kissing her. Of getting to have her in my arms like this. I fucking love this woman.

"C'mon. Let's go."

I set my beer down and turn off the TV before lifting Presley into my arms. Her kisses pepper my face and neck as a feverish need rolls through me.

We spend the night making love. Getting so wrapped up in one another, that I thank my lucky stars that we are here together.

I don't know what else I could ever need in my life. I have Presley. I have my kids. My family. The ranch.

This is everything I always wanted. And I couldn't be happier.

Want more in Pinecrest? Anything For You will be here on June 26, 2026! Preorder now!

Or if you want more small town, check out my Dixon Creek Ranch series now…available in audio and ebook!

Acknowledgments

Book thirty-three is out in the world!

It's hard to believe that the first book in my new small town series is here! I've been planning this series for so long that it's crazy to me that it's finally here. I hope you love this series and these characters as much as I loved writing them. Thank you to Tina and AmyLynn for beta reading and helping making this book perfect! Thank you to all my favorite people in my author world…Maria, Swati, Claire, Stephanie, Carrie…I love you all!

Thank you to all the readers who pick up my books and make this the best job in the world. You're the best!

Thank you for reading, and I hope to see you soon!
    <3 Emily

Also by Emily Silver

Pinecrest, Montana

Tequila & Cowboys - a newsletter freebie

Fight For Us

Anything For You - coming June 26, 2026

Falling Together - coming August, 2026

Dixon Creek Ranch

Yours to Take

Yours to Hold

Yours to Be

Yours to Forget

Yours To Lose

Yours To Love

For a complete list of all my books, please visit my website.

About the Author

Image by Tricia B @TheSmutFairy

USA Today Bestselling author Emily Silver was destined to be a writer after winning a Young Author award in second grade. She loves writing inclusive stories, with strong heroines and the swoony men who fall for them.

 A lover of all things romance, Emily started writing books set in her favorite places around the world. As an avid traveler, she's been to all seven continents and sailed around the globe.

 When she's not writing, Emily can be found sipping cocktails on her porch, reading all the romance she can get her hands on and planning her next big adventure!

 Find her on social media to stay up to date on all her adventures and upcoming releases!